There was a m_____ ___en I heard...yipes...I heard this grunting sound, and we're talking about grunts that were DEEP and powerful and so creepy that the hair stood up on the back of my neck. At first I thought it might have been a train or a bulldozer, but...no, that wasn't likely.

Gulp. I had a feeling that...you know, in all the excitement of Slim's bronc ride, I had more or less forgotten what had started it: Winkie, with the barn door on his horns. I think the men had forgotten too, but that rumble of grunts sent all our heads snapping around.

Winkie had been standing behind us the whole time and hadn't made a peep or moved a hair, but now...gulp...he began to stir. And all at once, in the back of my mind, I saw this flashing sign that said: *"Maybe you shouldn't have barked."*

WITHDRAWN

WITHDRAWN

The Case of the
Three Rings

John R. Erickson

Illustrations by Gerald L. Holmes

Maverick Books, Inc.

MAVERICK BOOKS, INC.
Published by Maverick Books, Inc.
P.O. Box 549, Perryton, TX 79070
Phone: 806.435.7611
www.hankthecowdog.com

First published in the United States of America by Maverick Books, Inc. 2014.

1 3 5 7 9 10 8 6 4 2

Copyright © John R. Erickson, 2014

All rights reserved

LIBRARY OF CONGRESS CONTROL NUMBER: 2014949511

978-1-59188-164-3 (paperback); 978-1-59188-264-0 (hardcover)

Hank the Cowdog® is a registered trademark of John R. Erickson.

Printed in the United States of America

Except in the United States of America, this book is sold subject
to the condition that it shall not, by way of trade or otherwise, be lent,
re-sold, hired out, or otherwise circulated without the publisher's
prior consent in any form of binding or cover other than that in which
it is published and without a similar condition including this
condition being imposed on the subsequent purchaser.

To the memory of our
dear friend, Bobby Barnett,
who left us much too soon.

CONTENTS

CHAPTER ONE

Attacked by a Charlie Monster with Vampire Teeth

It's me again, Hank the Cowdog. It was three o'clock in the morning, and dark. Suddenly, I heard an odd sound...several odd sounds...thuds and thumps. My head shot up and I raised Earatory Scanners. ES locked in on the sounds and confirmed the presence of a stranger in the house.

House? What house? Where was I? It didn't matter. I went into Stage Two of our Early Warning Protocol—opened my eyes.

Squinting into the gloomy half-light, I saw... good grief, there was a strange man, an intruder, creeping down the hall! He had...he had green skin and hair down in his eyes and HORNS GROWING OUT THE TOP OF HIS HEAD!

1

I did a quick assessment of the situation. I hate to do Red Alerts in the middle of the night, but there are times when a dog has no choice. I reached for the microphone of my mind and issued the alarm.

"Hank to Drover, over. We have a Charlie Monster creeping toward us down the hall, ETA in ten seconds. We're going straight into Ranch Red Alert, and this is not a drill. Repeat, *this is not a drill*. Battle stations!"

Moments later, Drover was standing beside me, wobbling on unsteady legs. I noticed right away that his eyes seemed crooked. I leaped to my feet and said, "Good, you're here. Are you awake?"

"Midget frigate spaghetti leaves."

"What?"

"Skittle rickie tattoo...where are we?"

I looked into the emptiness of his eyes. "I don't know, but you'd better snap out of it, soldier. We're in Ranch Red Alert and if you want to live long enough to see the sun rise, you'd better lay down some serious barks."

Just for a moment there was a gleam of recognition in his glazed eyeballs, then he did just what you'd expect Drover to do. He let out a squeak and wiggled himself underneath a coffee table.

Coffee table? That gave me my second clue in this case. We were in a house that had a coffee table, which meant we weren't on the porch or under the gas tanks.

Well, Drover had left me alone to face the intruder, which goes to prove that life isn't always fair. We don't always get what we want or deserve. If you're Drover, you can pick your battles. If you're Head of Ranch Security, you take everything they throw at you—the good, the bad, and the awful.

I filled my tanks with air, activated Hair Lift-up, took careful aim at the advancing Charlie, and began firing round after round of deafening barks. We're talking about the Big Ones, the kind that produce such a recoil, it throws a dog backward on each blast. Most dogs can't do more than three of those without losing their balance. I fired off six of them, one right after...

"Hank, dry up!"

Huh? Had the creature spoken my name? I was almost sure he had, but how could he have gotten my name? Had the Charlies hacked into our database and broken all our secret codes? Yes, our systems had been compromised and I found myself facing a terrible decision. Should I go down fighting for my ranch or save myself for another day?

I dived under the coffee table. "Move over, son, I'm coming in!"

I locked the hatch behind me, raised the periscope, and watched as the intruder went slouching into another room, perhaps the kitchen. That gave me the third clue in the case: wherever we were, it had a kitchen.

Behind me, I heard Drover's quivering voice. "Who is that?"

"Shh. We don't have a positive identification yet. Somehow he broke into the house and sneaked past our Warning Net."

"Whose house? Where are we?"

"Shhh. I don't know."

Drover blinked his eyes and glanced around. "Wait a second. I think we spent the night at Slim's place and maybe that's where we are."

"Drover, it's still dark and we can't be sure. Wait! Do you hear that?" We cocked our ears and listened. A refrigerator door opened and closed. Dishes clattered.

Drover let out a gasp. "Oh my gosh, he's stealing food!" All at once, a light came on in his eyes and a grin spread across his mouth. "Wait a second. Maybe it's Slim."

"What? Drover, this is no time for jokes. What I saw wasn't Slim."

"Yeah, but sometimes in the middle of the night, when his hair's a mess, he looks like a monster."

"Okay, pal, you think it's Slim? You go check it out."

"Me!"

"It was your idea. Go, move it!"

I pushed him out of the bunker and he tiptoed across the room. At the door that led into the kitchen, he stopped and peeked around the corner. A moment later, he dived back into the bunker.

"You're right, it's not Slim!"

"See? You need to listen to your superior officers. Any idea who it might be?"

His teeth were chattering. "I don't know, but he's nine feet tall and I think he has vampire teeth."

"Good grief. Do you think he might eat dogs?"

"Well, I don't know. He was eating something."

"Yes? And what was it? I need facts, Drover, facts and details."

He rolled his eyes around. "Well, let's see...oh yeah. I think it was a boiled turkey neck."

I stared at the runt. "A boiled turkey neck!"

"That's what it looked like."

I took a deep breath and climbed out of the bunker. "Drover, do you see what this means?"

"How can a turkey neck mean anything?"

"Please listen carefully." I stuck my nose in his face and raised my voice. "There's only one man in the whole world who would eat a cold, left-over, boiled turkey neck at three o'clock in the morning."

"Gosh, you mean..."

"Yes! What you saw in the kitchen was Slim Chance. He lives in this house. He sleeps in that bedroom down the hall. We see him every day.

He isn't nine feet tall, he doesn't have vampire teeth, and I can't believe you thought he was a monster."

"Well, you said it first, and you barked at him too."

"I did not bark at him. You're the one who…" I blinked my eyes and glanced around. "Drover, when this thing started, we were asleep, right?" He nodded. "In other words, our minds might not have been operating at full capacity?" He nodded.

I crept across the room and peeked into the kitchen, then returned to the spot where Drover was waiting. "It's Slim. He's eating a turkey neck. I'm canceling Ranch Red Alert."

"Oh good!"

"And Drover…" I moved closer and lowered my voice. "I think it would be best if we kept this to ourselves—you know, inside the Security Division."

"You mean…"

"Yes. That business about Slim being a Charlie Monster…ha ha…it's so ridiculous, we don't need to spread it around."

"Yeah, somebody might think we're just a couple of dumb dogs."

"Exactly, and think of what a bad effect that could have on morale. We must protect ourselves from lies and gossip."

"Yeah, even when they're true."

"Especially when they're true. Lies that contain a germ of truth can be very contagious, so here's our story: We heard dogs barking but it wasn't us. We don't know anything about anything. Got it?"

He grinned and gave me a wink. "Got it."

"Good! Now, let's go into the kitchen and see what's going on."

Okay, we'd had a little mix-up, a simple case of mistaken identity. Ha ha. But when a guy's jerked out of a deep sleep, he sometimes...anyway, let's back off and start all over again.

It must have been around the end of May. Wait. May comes in the spring, right? We were still in wintertime. It was the last day of December, New Year's Eve day to be exact, the very day that Slim and I learned a lot more about gathering buffalo than we ever wanted to know, but that comes later. At this point in the story, you're not supposed to know about the scary part.

You heard nothing about buffalo, right? Thanks.

Okay, Drover and I had spent the past week camped out at Slim's bachelor shack, two miles east of ranch headquarters. We often camped

8

there in the winter because Slim was kind enough to let us sleep inside the house, near his wood-burning stove.

See, our main office at ranch headquarters can be a little drafty in the dead of winter. I mean, sometimes I speak of it as "our Vast Office Complex," but the truth is, it consists of two old gunny sacks beneath a pair of three hundred gallon fuel tanks. No heater and no walls to stop the whistling north wind that often comes in the winter months.

I'm not whining or complaining, and I'm not going to say a word about Management being too CHEAP to build us the kind of office complex we deserve. I'm sure Loper had his reasons for putting the entire Security Division in a cramped, drafty little FLEABAG OF AN OFFICE beneath the gas tanks, although I can't imagine what they were.

On the other hand, Slim Chance, the hired hand on our outfit, had an enlightened policy about Dogs In The House, and in the depths of winter, we often chose to move the entire staff two miles down the creek to his place. There, in the Security Division's Winter Headquarters, we conducted ranch business in the living room, beside a big, friendly, wood-burning stove.

That's where we were on that Saturday morning, New Year's Eve day of whatever year it was, and the time had come for us to greet the Master of the House and find out what in thunder he was doing, wandering around the house at three o'clock in the morning.

You'll see. It was pretty strange.

CHAPTER TWO

Slim's Fateful Decision

~~~~~~

Drover and I were on our way to the kitchen to wish Slim the good-morningest of good mornings, when we met him coming into the living room. He had just finished gnawing on a cold turkey neck. He wore flannel pajamas, his hair was a mess, and there was an odd expression on his face: distracted and very serious.

The man had something on his mind and that was odd. I got the feeling that he'd been thinking about something during the night and we were fixing to hear about it.

I gave Drover the signal to cancel Happy Dog and Good Morning, and we shifted into a program called Dogs Who Listen. It's a dandy program but pretty difficult to pull off. It requires that we mirror the moods of our people, don't you see. If they look thoughtful, we look thoughtful. If they want to talk, we listen.

The reason it's a tough program is that it requires a high level of concentration. As you might expect, Drover isn't very good at that, because he has a lot of trouble staying on task. When we're doing Dogs Who Listen, we can't scratch or fall asleep. You'd be surprised at how crabby our people get when they confide in their dogs, and we scratch or fall asleep.

We sat down on the living room floor and waited to hear what this was all about. Wearing a deep scowl, Slim paced two circles around the room, then stopped beside the stove and stared at the floor. "Dogs, I can't sleep. A week ago, I done a terrible thing and it's eating me up."

Drover and I exchanged glances. What was this? Slim had done a terrible deed and we didn't know about it? I inched closer so that I could hear every word.

"I asked a fine lady if she'd marry me, and she said yes. Now my conscience won't give me a minute's peace. I think she was feeling sorry for me, is why she said yes, and I'm betting that she's changed her mind, only she's too nice to tell me."

He looked down at us. "I've been brooding

about it all week, and the truth just came to me. I've got nothing to offer Viola. She needs to forget about me and go on down the road. I'll wait till eight o'clock and then I'm going to call her up and tell her the deal's off. She'll probably cry for two minutes, but for the rest of her life, she'll thank the Lord that I let her off the hook."

He heaved a deep sigh. "There, the decision's made and maybe I can get some sleep." He shuffled off toward the bedroom. "Hank, if I ain't up by eight o'clock, bark me out of bed."

And with that, he was gone. I was too stunned to speak, and my mind drifted back to that day a week ago. Yes, I remembered it very well. In a snowstorm, Slim and I spent five hours gathering a hundred head of steers off a busy highway and driving them five miles back to the ranch. He was ahorseback, I was afoot, and Miss Viola drove ahead of us in the pickup. Fellers, that was one of those times when the weather wasn't fit for man nor beets. We're talking about brutal cold.

Slim caught a bad chill and came down with galloping pneumonia. Miss Viola had to drive him to the hospital (he fought it every step of the way, as you might expect). He slept most of the way into town and seemed to be out of his head with the fever, but all at once he sat up straight, looked at Viola with a crazy expression in his eyes, and said, "You know, me and you ought to get married some time." Then he went back to sleep.

I was right there in the cab of the pickup and saw the effect it had on Miss Viola. It made her so happy, she laughed and cried at the same time. She was afraid he wouldn't remember what he'd said, but two days later, when he got out of the hospital, he asked her again—and even slipped a lock washer on her ring finger (he didn't have an engagement ring). She cried with joy and threw her arms around his neck.

For a whole week, Drover and I had adjusted to the new reality. Slim had finally come to his senses and had done what every sane human and dog had known all along: that he should put a ring on that lady's finger and let her start planning for the future.

And now he was going to call her up and tell her the deal was off?

I couldn't believe it. I COULD NOT BELIEVE IT! Didn't he know that she'd been waiting for years for him to ask the Big Question? I mean, it was so obvious, even the dogs knew it.

Remember all the times she'd volunteered to help him haul hay and move cattle? All the dozens of cookies she'd baked for him? The times she'd taken care of him when he was hurt and sick, all the meals she'd cooked for him?

Any man with a brain in his head would have seen the glow on her face when she was around him, but Slim...oh brother! Sometimes the man drove me nuts. He had a treasure in his hands and now he was fixing to throw it away.

I turned to my assistant. "Drover, if he makes that phone call, I'll be forced to take drastic action."

Drover's gaze returned from the vapors. "Oh, hi. What's a plastic reaction?"

"If he backs out of the engagement, I'm going to bite him."

"Yeah, chewing plastic's kind of fun."

"I'll probably lose my job, but I don't care."

"You sure got in trouble for chewing the plastic handle on Sally May's garden trowel. Boy, she threw a fit."

"What? Viola threw a fit?"

"No, Sally May."

"Sally May threw a fit because Viola was chewing plastic? Drover, what are you talking about?"

He stared at the floor and shook his head. "I don't know. It's three o'clock in the morning and nothing makes sense. I'm going back to bed."

He shuffled over to his favorite spot in front of the stove, flopped down, curled up into a ball, and went right to sleep. What a weird little mutt.

Oh well. He'd been right about one thing. It was three o'clock in the morning and my bed was calling me back. I scratched around on the bare carpet, hoping to soften it up a bit (no luck there) and flopped down.

My body cried out for sleep, but I already mew that slop wooden crumb...sleep wouldn't come. My mind was just...purple onion Spanish rice chicken coop...my murg was just too wound up over that bushwhack with Slum...that business with Slim. If only the bananas wore cufflinks, the whooping cough wouldn't be any the wiser...murf bop pattywhack, give a dog a bone...snurf snicklefritz mulligan stew....zzzzzzzzzz.

Okay, maybe I finally drifted into a troubled sleep, after tossing and turning for hours and worrying myself sick over Slim Chance and his latest bonehead idea. The next thing I knew, it was morning. I was awakened by the sound of footsteps. I opened my eyes and saw...good grief! There was some kind of monster—nine feet tall, and he had vampire teeth and three horns sticking out...

Wait, hold everything. Ha ha. You can fool Hank the Cowdog once in a row, but never twice. It was Slim, dressed in flannel pajamas, and he didn't fool me, not even for a second. Okay, maybe for one second, but it was no big deal.

I rose to my feet, took a good stretch, and glanced around. Daylight was showing through the windows, so it must have been around eight o'clock. Wait! Hadn't Slim told me to do something at eight o'clock? My mind raced back to that strange encounter I'd had with him in the middle of the night.

Oh yes, he'd told me to bark him out of bed, but he was already out of bed, stumbling around the house and slurping on a cup of coffee. Should I bark anyway? Maybe so. I mean, a dog should follow orders, even when they seem pointless. I barked.

"Hank, dry up."

See how he is? He tells me to bark at eight o'clock, I bark, and he snarls at me to "dry up." Nobody understands how hard it is to be a dog around here.

He raked the hair out of his eyes and reached for the telephone, and now I remembered what he'd said in the middle of the night: he was going to call Miss Viola and tell her their engagement was off. And do you remember what I'd vowed to do if he made that call?

I had taken a solemn vow to BITE HIM, in hopes of preventing him from making the dumbest decision of his life. Through some miracle, he'd made the right move and asked her to marry him, and now he was on verge of blowing the whole deal to smithereens—*because he felt he wasn't good enough for her*!

How dumb was that?

Hmm. You know, come to think about it, he had a point. I don't mean to be cruel, but let's look at the facts. The guy had skinny legs, big feet, and a long nose. In the morning, he looked like a vampire. He ate boiled turkey necks and sandwiches made of ketchup and canned mackerel (that's really bad stuff). He seldom washed his dirty dishes and was prone to sing corny songs to his dogs.

You add that all up and you get...why was she interested in such a man? I mean, the evidence just screamed out the verdict: SHE WAS TOO GOOD FOR HIM!

In other words, Slim had arrived at a sensible decision and was fixing to do what any honorable man would have done, call her up and tell her that he'd made a terrible mistake. That left only one question unanswered: would she remain an old maid, or would she marry...well, ME, for example?

I'm not one to honk my own canoe, but while we're looking at evidence, let's pull out the file on me. Check this out:

- Long, handsome cowdog nose.
- A great set of ears.
- Wonderful personality, worlds of charm.
- A deep, manly aroma.
- A noble heart.
- Years of distinguished service heading up the ranch's Security Division.

Pretty impressive, huh? You bet. The only lady dogs in Texas who weren't wild about me were the ones who'd never met me, and that couldn't be helped. A dog can't be everywhere at once.

Did I deserve Miss Viola's love and devotion? Absolutely, you bet. But one small problem stood in our way. I was a dog, and there was no chance that she would ever marry me.

Sigh. What a bummer. Okay, back to Slim and his phone call.

The First Ring

Slim paced around the house like a caged coyote. He tugged on his chin, stared at the floor, waved a finger in the air, and muttered to himself.

"If I make this call, I'll be burning a bridge. It could change things forever, 'cause I don't think I'll ever meet another woman like her." He stopped and looked down at me. "Hank, I know I ain't worthy of such a lady, but...well, she seems to like me."

Yes, it was hard to explain.

"If she thinks I'm good enough, maybe I am... or could be." He began stalking around the room again. "I'm an honest man and a hard worker. I know I'm not wealthy..."

You're a pauper, but she doesn't seem to care.

"...but I'd try to give her the things she deserves." He stopped pacing, scowled at the floor, then looked at me again. "Hank, what should I do?"

You know, I had figured something out. If Slim never saw Viola again, *neither would I*, and you know how I felt about her. She was the sweetest, kindest woman I'd ever known. She was a great cook, a true friend, and she liked dogs, especially me. The thought that I might never see her again forced me to take charge of this deal.

Through wags, growls, and facial expressions, I gave him some fatherly advice.

"Meathead! For years, she's waited for you to come to your senses. For years, everyone on this ranch has been telling you that you'd better latch onto that lady, but did you listen? Oh no! And do you know why? Because inside your head, where the brain's supposed to be, you've got a big rock."

He gave me a peculiar look. "Are you growling at me?"

I plunged on, unable to control my emotions. "Yes, I'm growling at you, because you're worse than a meathead. You're a quitter! The lady is worth fighting for, so get off your tail, quit moping around like a sick calf, and act like a man. If you mess this up, pal, I will bite you every day for the rest of your life. I will howl all night long and you'll never get any sleep. I will chew your slippers and drag dead skunks into your yard."

Boy, I gave him the full load. I can't say that he understood every bit of it, but the expression on his face began to change. A look of steel came into his eyes. He glanced around the room and straightened his back.

We'll never know if he would have made that phone call, because he didn't get the chance. At that very moment, we heard the sound of a vehicle pulling up in front of the house.

"Huh. I wonder who that could be." He walked to the window and peeked through the dusty, moldy curtains that had been there since the Civil War. His eyes popped wide open and he let out a gasp. "Good honk, it's Viola!"

He must have realized that he was walking around in pajamas, and you know how cowboys are: they want everyone to think that they get up every morning at four-thirty and do chores by the light of a kerosene lantern. I don't know why, but they're all that way, and the last thing they ever want is for someone to catch them flopping around the house in pajamas at eight o'clock in the morning.

And you talk about a stampede! Slim wasn't exactly an electric personality first thing in the morning, but seeing Viola's pickup built a fire under him. He stepped on Drover, tripped on me, knocked over a chair, and went flying down the hall to his bedroom, where he began tearing off pajamas and pulling on jeans and a shirt.

He even managed to run a brush through his hair. Good. Now he didn't look so much like a vampire.

A moment later, there was a knock at the door. Slim had just enough time to button two buttons on his shirt before he opened the door. Oh, and get this. I noticed that he'd put on his shirt wrong-side out.

He threw open the door and...my goodness, there she stood, wearing a shy smile on her lovely lips. Slim stared at her (so did I, so did Drover) until he was able to say, "Why, Viola! What are you doing here?"

"May I come in? I won't be long."

"Well, sure, yes, come in. The house is kind of a mess, but...sit down."

She stepped inside and gave her head a shake. "I can only stay a minute."

"Is something wrong?"

She looked at him with clear blue eyes. "Slim, I don't know how to say this except to say it. I think we should call off the engagement."

Wow. You talk about DEAD SILENCE. You could have heard a flea crawling over the carpet. Slim couldn't have been more shocked if he'd seen a Martian. At last he was able to croak, "How come?"

She pressed her lips together and squeezed up a brave smile. "I'm honored that you asked, I really am. It made me very happy, but I don't think it will work." Tears filled her eyes and she bit her lip. "Let's face it. I'm not much of a catch. Now I have to go."

She whirled around and was on her way out the door when he grabbed her arm. "Wait, don't leave."

She gave her head a vigorous shake. "If I don't leave, I'll cry."

"That's okay, cry all you want."

She came back inside, flopped down in a chair with two recent issues of *Livestock Weekly* in the seat, buried her face in her hands, and cried. Slim stood beside her and patted her on the shoulder. "Did you say that you're not a good catch?"

She nodded and peeked out from behind her

hands. "Of course! I'm a silly old maid. I live with my parents and drive my daddy's ranch pickup. I'm not glamorous, fashionable, rich, or talented. For ten years every bachelor in the county has walked past me, even the ones that were older than Moses."

"Well, my dogs sure like you."

I couldn't believe he said that. What a clod! I mean, it was true, but what a dumb thing to say to a lady! It sent her into another burst of crying and left him wondering what to say next. Me? I was ready to bite his pockets off.

He fidgeted and shifted his feet and ran his gaze around the room, and finally said, "Let me tell you something." He told her about the phone call he had planned to make. "See, you got it all backwards. You're everything a man could want, and I'm just an old boot. It don't seem like a fair deal for you."

She brushed a tear away and looked up him. "You were going to tell me *that*?"

"Yes ma'am, only I didn't quite get around to it."

She broke into a laugh. "How funny! We've been engaged for a whole week, yet on the same day, each of us decided to call it off. That's funny." She glanced around the room. "Well, where does that leave us?"

Bewildered, Slim made his way over to his easy chair and sat down. "I don't have any more idea than a rabbit. One minute, I'm so scared I can't sleep, and the next, I'm too excited to sleep."

"Scared of what?"

"Everything—making a living, supporting a wife, changing my socks every day."

"Don't you suppose that most men have those fears? When it's done right, marriage is a big change."

"All I know is that you're causing me to lose a lot of sleep."

"Well, it shouldn't be so painful. Maybe we should just call it off. We can still be friends."

The steel returned to Slim's eyes and he leaned forward in his chair. "Yeah, but I don't want to be your friend. If I let you go, I'll be kicking myself for the rest of my life. I don't deserve a lady as fine as you, but if you'll have me, I'd sure like to be your..." He choked and coughed. "...husband."

She smiled. "Is it that hard to say?"

"Yes ma'am, it's going to take some practice."

She was thoughtful for a moment. "Here's an idea. You think about it all day. If you decide that we should do it, come for supper tonight at six. You can ask Daddy's permission."

Slim's eyes bugged out. "Ask Woodrow? You'd better hide his gun or he'll shoot me."

She laughed. "Oh fiddle, he will not. He's been trying to marry me off for years."

"Well...I guess we'll find out."

Viola's face grew solemn. "But remember, *you don't have to come*. If you don't, that will be your answer and I'll understand." She reached into the pocket of her coat and handed him the lock washer. "Here's your ring back. If you come tonight, we'll start from scratch. If you don't come...well, you'll have an extra lock washer."

"Does that mean you'll say yes?"

She gave her head a cute little toss. "I might. You won't know unless you show up."

"I'll be there, you can bet on it. All I have to do is feed cows today. I might even have time to take a bath."

She lifted one eyebrow. "You'd better!"

She got up to leave and he followed. At the door, he reached his arms around her and pulled her into a hug. "When you're around, everything feels right."

She pressed her cheek against his chest. "That's a good sign, don't you think?"

"Yes ma'am, I do."

"Slim, you've *got* to stop calling me 'ma'am.'"

"Yes ma'am."

She gave him a playful slap on the arm. "If you decide to come, bring your banjo. We'll play for Mother and Daddy. And your shirt is wrong-side out."

With that, she floated out into the cold morning air, leaving a hint of delicious perfume lingering in the room. It smelled a whole lot better than Slim's old boots.

CHAPTER FOUR

Uncle Johnny's
Bottle Calf

When Viola left the house, it was as if...well, it was like being in a big concert hall when the program's over. Everyone leaves, they turn out the lights, and there you are, standing in a dark shell. She had a kind of radiance that just filled up a room.

When she had gone, Slim did something really strange. He opened up his instrument case, brought out his banjo, sat down in his favorite chair, and sang a song. He sang a song to US, his dogs, and what's even more shocking, it was nice...pretty...a love song, if you can believe that.

You probably want to hear it, but we have to get on with the story. Maybe, if things turn out right, we can listen to it later on. But I'll tell you this: it wasn't bad.

Slim put his banjo back in the case and stared at the floor for a long time. "Well, we got that settled, and I *will* be at her house at six o'clock, even if her daddy tries to shoot me." Just then, the telephone rang. Slim's face fell into a scowl and he grumbled, "That's got to be Loper. What does he want?" He picked up the phone and held it away from his ear, so I was able to hear both sides of the conversation.

Loper said, "Did I get you out of bed?"

"Heck no, been up for hours. I was having some breakfast."

"You cooked breakfast?"

"That's right. Last week, I boiled up a pot of turkey necks. I keep 'em in the fridge and they make a dandy breakfast. You want me to save one for you?"

Loper barked a laugh. "No thanks. Listen, Uncle Johnny just called. He's got a little job and needs some help."

"A little job?"

"He said it won't take long. He's got a calf out in the neighbor's pasture. Why don't you saddle a horse and go help him. I'll feed the cows for you."

Slim rocked up and down on his toes. "Loper,

Uncle Johnny's 'little jobs' have a way of turning into big jobs. I've got someplace to go tonight and I need to be back here by four o'clock."

"A New Years party?"

"Not exactly."

"Where? Is Viola going?"

Slim's face turned red. "I ain't talking."

Loper laughed. "Holy cow, you've got a date and you're going to a New Year's party! I can't believe this! What's the world coming to? Well, have fun with Uncle Johnny."

Slim hung up the phone and glared at the floor. "I didn't need this, not today. The last time I helped that old goat, I didn't get home till after dark." He shot a glance at me. "But this time I will."

Half an hour later, the sun had climbed over the eastern horizon and Slim was ready to go, dressed for a winter day ahorseback: shotgun chaps, denim jacket over a wool vest, a wild rag around his neck, and his high-top riding boots with spurs attached. Oh, and he'd brought his wind-up alarm clock from the house and set it on the dash of the pickup.

Ordinarily, Slim wasn't a slave to the clock, but today he was watching the time. Good.

He hooked up the sixteen-foot stock trailer

and saddled a young horse called Socks (he had three white feet). When he loaded Socks into the trailer, he was ready to go. I followed him to the pickup door.

Where was Drover? Sitting on the porch, watching. He'd said the cold ground hurt his feet and he didn't want to go. Oh brother.

When Slim reached for the door handle, he saw me standing at his feet. "Are you follering me?"

Well, sort of, yes. That's what loyal dogs do.

"You can't go. I've got work to do and you'd get in the way."

Yes sir. I understood.

"Bye. I know you'll miss me."

He climbed into the pickup and slammed the door, shifted into first gear and drove away.

Maybe you think it's pretty sad that a cowboy would go off on a big adventure and leave his faithful dog behind, but don't waste any time feeling sorry for me. See, I had tricks that Slim didn't know about. Hee hee.

He'd gotten all the way to the mailbox before he noticed that I was following him. He stopped and rolled down his window. "Hank, go home!"

Yes sir.

He turned right on the county road and picked

up speed. After a bit, he glanced into his side mirror and saw me sprinting beside the trailer. He slammed on the brakes, jumped out, and started throwing rocks at me.

"Hammerhead, GO HOME!"

He chunked three rocks and missed every time. He jumped back inside the pickup and drove off again. Hee hee. I followed, and boy, did that make him mad! I knew it would, but, well, what's a dog supposed to do?

He stopped again and I could hear him sputtering inside the cab. He got out and glared at me for a long time. "Hank, you are the most disobedient, ill-trained, ungrateful whelp of a dog I ever saw. I told you to go home."

Yes, I knew that but...well, I really wanted to go with him and I was pretty sure that, deep in his heart, he wanted me to go too.

He picked up a big rock and threw it with all his might. It missed me but did something to his back. He started walking like...I don't know, like a crab or something, and screamed, "Now look what you've done!"

Well, I was sorry he'd hurt his back, but maybe he should stop throwing rocks at his dog.

He rubbed his back, shook his head, kicked a weed, rolled his eyes up to the sky, opened the door, and pointed inside. "Get in here!"

Oh happy day! I dashed to the pickup and leaped inside, taking my usual place of honor beside the shotgun-side window.

You'd have to say that the atmosphere inside the cab was a little frosty for the first two miles. Slim's glare went back and forth, from the road to me, and I could hear him fuming under his breath. I knew he would find his voice eventually and that I would have to listen to him gripe and roar. Sure enough...

"One of these days, pooch, you're going to pull that trick and I ain't going to stop. You'll follow me five miles and get tired, and then you'll be lost, and I won't go looking for your sorry hide. You know what I'll do?"

Uh...no.

"I'll celebrate! Yes sir, I'll invite all the neighbors and cook a goat, and after we're done eating, I'll stand up on a chair and make a speech. I'll say, 'I'm proud y'all could come and help me celebrate this happy occasion, 'cause today I have got rid of a dog that wasn't worth eight eggs.'"

He snapped his head at me, then went back to his main job, keeping the pickup out of the ditches.

Well, he'd vented his spleen, all right, and it

had sounded pretty stern, but I knew something about Slim that he didn't know about himself. An hour later, he would have forgotten the whole thing and he'd be glad to have me along.

I'm not saying that a dog should make a habit of being disobedient or that it's a good pattern to establish. It's not. All I'm saying is that sometimes our people don't know what's good for them, and a dog has to...well, take charge.

So off we went to Uncle Johnny's place. He lived up on the flat country, about fifteen or twenty miles northwest of our ranch. Most of the snow we'd gotten on Christmas day had melted off, leaving just a few drifts in the ditches.

Uncle Johnny and his wife Marybelle had a tidy place that consisted of a small white house, a steel round-top barn, and a set of working corrals. We turned off the highway and drove down a lane with barbed wire fences on both sides.

Uncle Johnny, you might recall, was Sally May's uncle, a small, feisty man who carried some age, maybe seventy years or more. When we got there, he was sitting in an old flatbed pickup, smoking a pipe and reading the Twitchell newspaper.

Slim got out of the pickup and gave me a

glare. "If I let you out, can you act halfway civilized?"

Oh yes sir, no problem. I was honored to be there and sure didn't want to be a burden.

"Okay, get out and try not to act your IQ. If they've got any chickens, buddy, you'd better leave 'em alone. Aunt Marybelle might not be as soft-hearted as I am."

Yes sir. I hopped out and switched all circuits over to Perfect Dog.

Slim walked over to Johnny's pickup, his spurs jingling on the gravel. They exchanged greetings and talked about the weather and the price of feed. Then Slim said, "Johnny, before we get started, I want you to know that I have to be gone from here at three o'clock. I've got a meeting tonight and can't be late."

Johnny folded up the paper and pitched it up on the dashboard. "Who has meetings on New Year's eve?"

"It don't matter. The point is, I have someplace to go."

Johnny chuckled and gave Slim a sideways glance. "What's her name?"

"Yankee Doodle Dandy. Now, what's this job I'm supposed to help you with? Loper said something about a calf."

Johnny nodded and pointed the stem of his pipe to the north. "Bull calf found a hole in the fence and went neighboring. I see you brought a horse."

"That's what the boss said to do."

"We won't need a horse. This calf's as gentle as a pup. We call him Winkie. I raised him on a bottle and he's kind of a pet. We can show him a feed sack and he'll follow us all the way home. Get in, we'll take my pickup."

"What about Hank? I didn't invite him but he came anyway."

Uncle Johnny looked down at me and smiled. "Bring him. We like dogs around here. He can ride up front with us." And off we went to find Winkie.

CHAPTER FIVE

We Lock Winkie In The Barn

We had driven a mile to the north, when Johnny stopped the pickup and pointed to a herd of black cows in a pasture. "There he is, the brown one."

Slim squinted his eyes and studied the cattle. "Hey Johnny, that's not a *calf*. He's bigger than the cows."

"Yes, well, Winkie grew up. When you bottle-feed 'em twice a day, you don't notice."

"Uh huh. Well, you're right, Winkie grew up." Slim leaned forward and took a closer look. "Hey Johnny, that thing looks like...a buffalo!"

"Oh yes, he's my pet buffalo. Loper didn't tell you?"

For a moment, Slim seemed lost in thought.

"I'm sure it just slipped his mind. So we're fixing to gather a full-grown buffalo bull, is that right?"

"Well, he's only two years old and still has some growing to do."

"But he weighs about fifteen hundred pounds and has a real big set of horns."

Johnny swatted the air with his hand. "Oh, don't worry about them horns. He never uses 'em for anything but scratching at flies."

Slim stared off into the distance. "I just figured out how come Loper was so anxious to feed cows today."

Uncle Johnny pointed to a wire gate. "Open that gate and leave it open. We'll be coming back this way." He must have noticed that Slim's expression had soured. "Now Slim, don't fret. This won't take long, and it'll be easy as pie. You'll see."

Slim opened the gate and we drove north to the herd of cows—and got a good look at Winkie. He might have been "a cute little bottle calf" at one time, but what we saw was a shaggy beast with a huge head, a hump in his back, a set of sharp horns, and a pair of deep black eyes that were looking us over when we came to a stop.

Uncle Johnny glowed with pride. "That's my Winkie. Watch this." He got out of the pickup and held out two pellets of feed in the palm of his hand. Winkie lumbered over, sniffed his hand, and ate the feed. Johnny laughed. "What do you say now, Slim? Didn't I tell you?"

Slim said nothing, but I could see that he wasn't convinced. Neither was I.

Uncle Johnny told Slim to drive the pickup back to the house, while Johnny sat on the tail gate and held out cubes of feed. Sure enough, Winkie trotted along behind us, through the wire gate, down a mile of dirt road, and all the way back to Uncle Johnny's corral.

An hour after we'd arrived, Uncle Johnny's pet buffalo was standing in the corral, munching

cubes of feed and swishing his short tail. Uncle Johnny was tickled. He rubbed his hands together and said, "Now, wasn't that easy?"

"Yes sir. In fact, it was so easy, it makes me wonder how come you needed me."

"Well, I needed someone to open the gate and drive the pickup." He frowned and pulled on his ear. "And sometimes Winkie don't like to stay penned up."

Slim stared at him. "Oh really?"

At that very moment, we heard a crash behind us. We all turned toward the sound and saw that Winkie had just built a new gate in Johnny's corral—he'd jumped into the middle of a panel made of tube steel and had left an impression of his body in the two top rails. In other words, he'd pretty well destroyed a steel panel, and he'd done it without much effort.

And now he was trotting north down the road, going right back to the pasture where we'd found him. Johnny wagged his head. "I never dreamed he'd do that twice in a row."

"He did it before?"

"Oh yeah, that's how he got with those cows."

"I thought you said he 'went through the fence'. You didn't mention that he wrecked it."

Johnny shook his head. "He was always such

a nice calf. I never dreamed...I guess he just don't like being in a pen."

"I guess he don't. Now what?"

Uncle Johnny rubbed his chin and gave it some thought. "Well sir, my neighbor sure wants Winkie out of that pasture. I mean, the man is seriously upset. We may need to use that horse after all."

"Johnny, this might sound like a dumb question, but if we get Winkie penned again, what's to keep him from going over the corral fence again?"

Johnny grinned and tapped himself on the temple. "I've already got that covered. This time, we'll put him in the barn and close the door."

Slim grunted and checked the angle of the sun. "What time is it?"

Uncle Johnny squinted at his watch. "I don't have my glasses."

Slim grabbed his wrist and looked at the watch. "It's one o'clock. At three, I'm gone. Let's get this done."

And with that, we all loaded into Slim's pickup-trailer rig and drove north, following the elusive Winkie.

We arrived at the pasture where the cows were grazing, just in time to see Winkie jump over the neighbor's barbed wire fence, and we're talking about a flat-footed jump without any kind of a running start. One second, he was sniffing the five-wire fence and the next second, he was on the other side, trotting toward the cows. And he didn't even touch the top wire.

Uncle Johnny smiled. "It's kind of amazing, how he can do that."

"Yes it is, and Johnny, it brings to mind a question." Slim gave him a hard look. "What in the world are you doing, trying to keep an animal that can flatfoot a five-wire fence? There ain't a fence in the whole Panhandle that could turn Winkie, if he didn't want to be turned."

Johnny heaved a sigh. "Well sir...I'm attached to him and can't bear the thought of giving him up."

Slim shook his head and gazed out the window. "Well, what's your plan this time?"

Johnny gave that some heavy thought. "Unload your horse and ride around behind him. Maybe you can ease him away from the cows. I'll drive the pickup and honk the horn. With me in front and you behind, maybe we can steer him back home."

"Should I take the dog?"

Johnny's eyes popped wide open. "Oh no, don't

46

show him a dog. Winkie don't like dogs at all. I mean, he goes nuts around a dog."

Yipes. Well, that was good to know, and it didn't even hurt my feelings, seeing as how I didn't have any use for a buffalo. Winkie and I would get along just fine, with me in the pickup and him outside.

Johnny opened the wire gate and we drove out into the pasture, where Winkie had rejoined the cows. Slim unloaded his horse, tightened the cinches, stepped up into the saddle, and rode north in a trot.

Once in the herd, he slowed to a walk and went to work. Uncle Johnny and I watched him. Slim was good at this and had a soft touch with livestock. He eased his horse through the herd, never got out of a long walk and didn't get the cattle stirred up. One by one, he eased the cows out of the herd and pushed them north, until Winkie was all by himself.

That's when Slim's horse took a closer look at the animal he was about to drive back to the barn. When he caught a whiff of Winkie's scent, he snorted and tried to quit the country. I mean, he was no dummy and he knew that shaggy thing wasn't a normal cow. Slim had to calm him down and do some persuading with his spurs.

Then he raised his right hand and made a circular motion. It meant, "Roll 'em!" Johnny started the pickup, honked the horn, and we drove south, back to the barn, watching Slim and the buffalo in the side mirror. Winkie trotted along behind us, with Slim bringing up the rear, just in case Winkie got any funny ideas.

Johnny nodded and smiled. "Now, that's how it's done. Old Slim makes a hand." His gaze landed on me. "I just wonder who he's got a date with tonight. I'd pay five dollars to know, but he'll never tell. I'll bet it's old Woodrow's daughter, you reckon?"

I gave him a blank stare and thumped my tail on the seat. Hey, if Slim wasn't talking, neither was I. We dogs know how to keep a secret—and believe me, we have plenty of them. If dogs wrote the history books...well, never mind, but it would make pretty interesting reading, and it would raise a lot of eyebrows.

That drive back to the barn was long and slow. We crept along at about five miles an hour, but at last we made it to the lane. Johnny kept a close watch in the side mirror and when he saw that Slim and the buffalo had gotten into the lane, he sped up and parked in front of the barn.

When he stepped out, he leaned into the open

window and gave me a hard glare. "You stay inside, Shep. We don't need any wrecks."

Well, sure, and neither did I. I had plenty of things to do without getting crossways with a buffalo.

Johnny hurried into the barn and came out with a bale of hay. He cut the twine and scattered the hay in a line from outside the barn, through the big overhead door, and then inside. By that time, Slim had arrived with Winkie, and right away the buffalo caught a whiff of the hay.

Johnny called him, making a cattle call: "Wooooo! Come on, son, come to feed, fresh bright alfalfa."

The buffalo went to the hay and started eating. Uncle Johnny eased toward the beast and patted him on the shoulder, then flashed a grin at Slim. "He's big but he's just some old cow's calf. Well, that's it, we've closed the deal. You hold him here. I'll park your rig at the end of the lane, block the road, see, just in case he tries to go back to the cows."

Slim nodded that he understood the plan. Johnny drove the pickup north and parked it sideways in the road, blocking it to all traffic. Once again, he told me to stay in the pickup. Maybe he thought I wasn't smart enough to remember that he'd already told me that.

Of course I would stay in the pickup! When my life gets so dull that I need some excitement, I'll chew on an electric wire. I WON'T parade myself in front of a buffalo bull that hates dogs. Sometimes these people...oh well.

Johnny hiked back to the barn, and together, he and Slim eased Winkie through the overhead door and into the barn. Johnny pulled on a rope that was attached to the door and it came sliding down. He turned a handle that locked it in place, brushed his hands together, and beamed a smile at Slim, who was still ahorseback.

"There it is, Slimbo, that's how you gather a buffalo."

Well! We had finished our job. Winkie was safe in the barn, I was alone in the pickup, and my reason for staying cooped up had just expired. See, I'd been in there a long time and all at once I had begun to notice...well, "the call of nature," as Slim would say.

Uncle Johnny had been kind enough to leave the window down on the driver's side, so I hopped up on the window ledge, balanced myself for a few seconds, and made a graceful dive to the ground.

There, I made a dash to the left front tire and

gave it a thorough sniffing. While I worked, I listened to the men talking in the distance. They were fifty yards away, but I could hear their voices as clear as a bell.

Uncle Johnny said, "Didn't I tell you it would be easy as pie?"

"I admit I had some doubts."

"With buffalo, it's all about how you approach 'em. You can't crowd 'em, see, 'cause when a buffalo don't want to be somewhere, he won't be there for long."

"I see," said Slim. "And how do they feel about barns?"

"Slim, as long as I keep hay and water in there…"

I didn't hear the rest of Uncle Johnny's Lesson on Buffaloes, and neither did anyone else, because at that very moment, his voice got lost in a loud CRASH. It was so loud, I jumped two feet in the air and, well, sent Secret Encoding Fluid spraying in all directions.

I whirled around, looked toward the barn, and witnessed an incredible spectacle.

CHAPTER SIX

Maybe I Shouldn't Have Barked

Something large, brown, and shaggy had just walked out of the barn, and it appeared to be WEARING HALF OF THE BARN DOOR ON HIS HEAD!

Have you figured it out? That was Winkie, Uncle Johnny's pet buffalo, and I guess he didn't like staying in the barn. He'd walked right through the overhead door and had a big section of sheet metal skewered on his horns. He was as blind as a bat and tossing his head to get rid of the piece of the door that was stuck to his horns.

But that was only the first part of the drama. The second part was...can you imagine what a young horse would think if he saw a buffalo clanking around with a barn door on his head?

Socks was pretty calm by nature and had a nice, quiet disposition under ordinary circumstances, but he got over that real quick. When he saw Winkie clanking around and coming towards him, he lost his mind. His ears shot up, his eyes bugged out, he snorted and ran sideways, flattened Aunt Marybelle's yard fence, and went to bucking like a National Finals bronc—through the yard and around the house.

Well, you know me. When my cowboy gets caught in a storm, I don't just stand around looking simple. I hit Turbo Six and went streaking up the road to the barn, but you'll be proud to know that I didn't bark. See, when a horse blows up, a barking dog very seldom helps the situation.

Oh, and don't forget what Uncle Johnny had said: Winkie wasn't fond of dogs, so I, uh, felt this would be a good time to keep silent.

Anyway, Socks bucked across the front lawn and was heading round the south side of the house. The front door flew open and out stepped Aunt Marybelle, Uncle Johnny's wife. She stared in open-mouth amazement and let out a scream. "Slim Chance, get that horse out of my yard!" Then a look of horror came over her face. "Slim, watch out for the clothesline!"

Uh oh. All eyes turned toward the north side

of the house where a bunch of wet clean clothes were flapping on two clotheslines. Have we ever discussed horses and clotheslines? Bad combination. You should never ride a bucking horse through a yard with a clothesline.

But this deal had moved way beyond Slim's control. He had a double handful of bronc and was doing well just to stay aboard. He was making a good ride, but this appeared to be one of those situations when a cowboy can't decide if he's better off staying in the saddle or getting bucked off.

When he disappeared around the back side of the house, he was still ahorseback and for several seconds I lost visual contact. I could hear some amazing snorts and grunts coming from Socks, and Slim yelling, "Whoa, Socks, easy boy!" When they came around the northeast corner of the house, Slim was still aboard...and Socks was highballing it straight toward the clotheslines.

He hit them with a full head of steam. Wires snapped, clothes flapped, and Slim's horse came out wearing the whole mess. He looked like a float in a parade and was pitching harder than ever. Right before he flattened another section of the yard fence, Marybelle screeched, "Watch out for my fence!"

Well, that was a good suggestion. It just didn't work out too well.

By this time, Socks had left the yard and had gotten back to the gravel drive in front of the barn. He was dragging two strands of clothesline wire and all of Marybelle's laundry, and he had somebody's denim work shirt draped over his face. That might have been the only thing that saved Slim from a terrible fate.

See, the horse was spooked out of his mind but also blinded by the shirt, and instead of bucking some more, he stopped in his tracks. For several seconds, nobody moved. Socks was trembling all over and heaving for air. So was Slim, and his face had turned the color of chalk.

It was an eerie moment. As quiet as a mouse, Slim swung his right leg over the cantle and stepped out of the saddle. He staggered a couple of steps, blinked his eyes, and checked to see if he had lost his hat. Of course he had. It had come off on the first jump.

He reached for the Leatherman tool he carried in a little pouch on his belt. It was the kind device that folded out into several tools: a pair of pliers, two sizes of screwdriver, a file, a little saw blade, and a can opener. He used the pliers to cut the clothesline wire and started removing laundry

from the horse. He talked in a quiet voice and gave Socks a pat now and then, and the horse stood still, but shaking all over. When Slim removed the shirt from the horse's face, he heaved a sigh of relief.

Whew! It appeared that the ordeal was over, and boy, what a wreck it had been.

Well, this seemed a good time for me to step in and take charge of the situation, and what could be more important than finding and retrieving Slim's hat? You know how these cowboys are about their hats. Without a hat, they feel undressed, out of costume, you might say, and I was pretty sure that Slim would be thrilled if I showed up with his hat.

It might even earn me a free turkey neck. I wasn't wild about his turkey necks and they were no substitute for a good steak, but those neck bones were pleasant to chew and in hard times, I'll never turn down a turkey neck.

So I made a dash to the yard, where his hat lay in the grass. With care and tenderness, I picked it up in my powerful jaws. If an ordinary mutt had attempted this, he would have left tooth tracks on the brim, and maybe slobber marks too. Not me. Hey, cowdogs understand cowboys, and the first thing you need to know about a cowboy is *don't mess with his hat.*

You can spill paint on his clothes, shave his head, hide his boots, burn his house down, and wreck his pickup, but *don't mess with his hat.* Your average cowboy spends a lot of time, shaping that hat so that it tells the world...to be honest, I'm not sure what it tells the world, but he's very fussy about the tilt of the brim and the crease in the crown. If you change the shape a cowboy's hat, you're shopping for trouble.

I knew that, so in picking up Slim's hat, I exercised the greatest of care and handled it as though it were a crown made of gold. His face bloomed into a smile when he saw me trotting toward him, a loyal cowdog delivering his master's most treasured possession.

"Well, look at this! Thanks, pooch." He took the hat, turned it around, and gave it a close inspection. "But next time, try not to slobber on it."

What? I did not slobber on it! In fact, I had gone to great lengths NOT to slobber on it. What does it take to please these people? I was so outraged, I barked.

Oops.

There was a moment of dead silence. Then I heard...yipes...I heard this grunting sound, and we're talking about grunts that were DEEP and powerful and so creepy that the hair stood up on the back of my neck. At first I thought it might have been a train or a bulldozer, but...no, that wasn't likely.

Gulp. I had a feeling that...you know, in all the excitement of Slim's bronc ride, I had more or less forgotten what had started it: Winkie, with the barn door on his horns. I think the men had forgotten too, but that rumble of grunts sent all our heads snapping around.

Winkie had been standing behind us the whole time and hadn't made a peep or moved a hair, but now...gulp...he began to stir. And all at once, in the back of my mind, I saw this flashing sign that said: *"Maybe you shouldn't have barked."*

It appeared that Winkie had gotten tired of wearing the overhead door, and to get rid of it, he proceeded to give his head several powerful shakes. There is nothing subtle about a buffalo bull and everything he does has an exaggerated effect. Winkie had a big head that was connected to a huge muscular neck, and when he shook his head, he was also tossing around a six-foot-by-three-foot panel of sheet metal—I mean, like a cat shaking a mouse.

At that point, things happened in a blur. The sheet metal flew off Winkie's horns and landed right in front of Socks, who had just recovered from his first nervous breakdown and went straight into his second. His eyeballs grew as big as pies, his ears went to the top of the flagpole, and fellers, he sold out—tore the reins out of Slim's hand and bucked a straight line into the barn.

I had just gotten over that surprise when I noticed...WINKIE WAS STARING AT ME...and he was making those deep grunting noises again and...yipes, shoveling up dirt with his front hooves.

Have you ever been stared at by a buffalo? There is nothing in those eyes that a dog wants to see. We're talking about cold black eyes that can freeze your gizzard.

In the spooky silence, Uncle Johnny whispered, "Slim, you'd better move away from the dog. I have an idea that Winkie's fixing to come uncorked."

Slim began backing away from me. The grunting sound in Winkie's throat had turned into a rumble of thunder and I could hear his front hooves tearing the ground like a backhoe and...

You know, at once I felt...well, very exposed, and when a dog is seized by the impulse of fear, he naturally wants to...well, seek the warmth and companionship of his human friends. Drawing my tail up between my legs, I began edging toward...

"Hank, get away from me!"

...the man I had loved and admired for so many years.

"Meathead, get back!"

You know, there's a very special bond between a cowboy and his dog. I mean, we guard his porch, ride in his pickup, sleep in his bed, drink out of his commode, share his sorrows...

"Hank!"

Why was he backing away from me, and screeching? Hey, that buffalo had a BAD look in his eyes and I needed a friend and a place to hide, so I went to Full Flames on all engines and took refuge behind...uh...the legs of my friend.

CHAPTER SEVEN

Winkie Does
Some Damage

Okay, let's get something straight before we move into the dark and scary parts of this story. If I'd had time to think about the situation, I *wouldn't* have taken refuge behind Slim's legs.

In the first place, he had skinny legs that offered about as much protection as a pair of toothpicks. If you're running from a buffalo, take refuge behind something made of concrete and rebar, not the bird-legs of a cowboy.

In the second place, I never dreamed that Slim would...well, trip over me and fall to the ground. Honest. It never entered my mind, and when he hit the ground, I felt terrible about it— so bad that I forgot about everything else and rushed to administer Healing Licks to his...

"Get away from me!"

Why was he pushing me away? And screaming? Gee, had all our years together come down to this? I was crushed. Hey, I'd invested my whole life in this guy and it just about broke my heart when he...

Huh?

The earth beneath my feet seemed to be trembling. I cocked one ear and heard...that was odd. Did we have trains around here? I didn't think so, but I was almost sure that I'd heard...

Gulk.

Did you forget about Winkie? I did. How could an intelligent dog forget about a snorting killer buffalo that was back-hoeing dirt only ten feet away from him? That's a great question and I have no great answer. All I can say is that... well, we cowdogs have tender feelings, even though we try to hide them most of the time, and when our friends take a tumble...uh oh.

HERE CAME WINKIE!

Just for an instant, time seemed to stop and my mind held a snapshot of something huge, shaggy, mad, and dangerous coming straight at me. And I heard this voice inside my head: "Bud, you'd better get out of here...fast!"

Out of the cornea of my eye, I saw Slim roll up

into a ball and cover his head with his arms. I also saw an enormous animal with sharp horns and a real bad attitude about dogs. I pushed the throttle to the floor and went to Full Afterburners.

Behind me, I heard Uncle Johnny yell, "Winkie, come back here! Be nice!"

Yeah, right. Be nice. What a joke.

You know, in many ways buffalo look and act like cows, but we should point out a few important differences. First, buffalo have amazing acceleration. They can go from a dead stop to full gallop in the blink of an eye.

Second, over a short distance they can run as fast as a horse. Your average ranch dog can stay ahead of a cow without a whole lot of effort, and can even look back and bark a little trash. With buffalo, you run for your life and don't even consider barking trash.

Third, this buffalo had some kind of twisted hatred of dogs. I mean, cows don't like dogs, but multiply that times ten and you get Winkie. What had I ever done to him? Nothing. I'd never even seen him until today, but fellers, he hated my guts and wanted to wear a few of them on his horns. And he wasn't kidding.

While I ran circles around the gravel drive in front of the barn, Slim and Uncle Johnny took to their heels and scattered like chickens. I mean, Winkie cleared the arena and was gaining ground on me and I could feel his blow-torch breath on my tail, so I feinted left and turned right, and went sprinting north down the lane.

I headed straight for Slim's pickup-trailer rig that was blocking the road. That would be my salvation...if I could stay alive that long.

Oh, what a chase! You should have seen it. I had become Rocket Dog. Grown trees bent to the ground in the wake of my jet engines. Dust swirled, fence posts shuddered, birds fell from the sky, stunned by the sonic booms.

Even so, Winkie was closing the gap on me and I could feel his blow torch burning the hairs on my tail. My legs ached and my lungs burned, my entire body begged for relief.

But fifty feet away from the pickup, I knew I was going to win this deal! If the race had gone another hundred feet, he would have rolled me and...I didn't even want to think about the rest of what might have happened. But the important thing is that I made it to the pickup and went sailing through the open window.

Oh yeah! I'd made it! I was alive!

And at that point, I did what any normal American dog would have done. I whirled around and cut loose with a withering barrage of barking. "Hey Winkie, you're pathetic! What a loser! I saw your momma walking down the street the other day and she was so ugly..."

CRASH!

I never would have dreamed that a buffalo would try to jump through a pickup window, but THERE HE WAS!

You've seen stuffed buffalo heads hanging on walls, right? That's what I was looking at, only this one wasn't stuffed. Lucky for me, he didn't get all the way inside the cab. I mean, the shoulders and hump of a buffalo won't fit through a pickup window, but he'd gotten enough of his head inside to scare the living bejeebers out of me.

"Hey, Winkie, what I said about your mother... it was childish and cruel and I'm really ashamed..."

He let out a thunderous, bellowing ROAR. I hit the floor and against the door. Hey, that rhymes, doesn't it? Roar, floor, door. Never mind. All I cared about was getting as far away from that dragon as I could.

For a long moment of heartbeats, I waited to see if he would come through the window. If he did, he would have no chance to kill me because I would already be dead from fright. He didn't come into the cab (whew!) but he sure messed up

the pickup. When he backed out, things made out
of glass and metal made a bunch of bad sounds.

Well, there stood the fifteen hundred-pound
Winkie. He snorted, flicked his ears, swished his
tail, and glanced off to the north. This next part
was hard to believe but I was there as a witness.
*He jumped onto the hood of the pickup, mashed it
like a bean can, jumped off the other side, and
headed north in a trot.*

As I watched him trotting away, the windshield
through which I was looking began to crack and
disintegrate, and I absorbed a powerful lesson
that had come from this experience. When
herding a buffalo, don't ever assume that you can
stop him by blocking the road with a pickup and

trailer. It won't stop him and he might destroy the pickup.

With broken glass falling like snow, I stood there, shaking from head to toenail. I heard footsteps approaching. It was Slim, running as fast as he could in his chaps and spurs. The man was obviously worried sick that his loyal companion had been maimed or killed. He would be SO GLAD to find that I was okay! I would have leaped out of the pickup and rushed out to meet him only I wasn't sure my legs would work.

Thirty feet away, he slowed to a walk, then stopped. His mouth dropped open as he leaned forward and stared at...well, what was left of his pickup, I guess. Uncle Johnny arrived just then, huffing and puffing.

He shook his head and heaved a weary sigh. "Well, I guess that settles it. You'd better rope him."

Slim's head snapped around and for a long moment, he stared at Uncle Johnny. "*Rope him!*"

"Well, yes. I hate to do it, but we've tried everything else."

Slim started laughing and couldn't stop. He laughed so hard, his face turned red. Finally he was able to speak. "Johnny, let me see if I can explain this. First of all, that horse of mine will never get within half a mile of a buffalo for the rest of his life, and if he does, he'll be bucking wide open in the opposite direction. In the second place, I might look dumb enough to pitch a loop on something that wrecks pickups, but I'm not."

Johnny shrugged. "Well, you read about men roping buffalo."

"Yes, and the message is always the same. *Don't try this!*"

"What about Winkie? He's going right back to those cows and my neighbor's sure going to be unhappy."

"Johnny, the only way you're going to get that buffalo gathered is to take all the cows with him. *Hire five good cowboys to do it.*"

Johnny squinted at the pickup and flinched. "Boy, he done a number on your pickup."

"The pickup belongs to your niece's husband and I can guarantee that when he sees it, he won't be proud of me or you or Winkie. In fact, he may have trouble deciding which one of us he wants to kill first."

Johnny gave his head a sad shake. "I just don't understand what got into Winkie. He's never acted this naughty."

Slim's gaze turned to him, and it seemed none too friendly. "What got into Winkie is that he's a

71

buffalo. He ain't a goldfish or a parakeet. He used to be a bottle calf, but now he's a wild animal that weighs fifteen hundred pounds."

Johnny pushed his hat back and scratched the top of his head. "Well, he was fine till your dog barked."

"Johnny, turn up your hearing aid and listen. Before my dog made a sound, your buffalo flattened a steel corral panel, jumped a five-wire fence, and walked through your barn door. We're lucky to be alive. Winkie needs a new home. Give him to a zoo. Tell 'em to send a fully covered, reinforced stock trailer that he can't destroy. Or I can come back tomorrow and we'll gather him with a .30-.06."

I think Slim was joking, but Uncle Johnny didn't laugh. He rocked up and down on his toes and chewed on his lip. "I hate to say this, but Marybelle's been telling me this for six months."

"Marybelle was right. What time is it?"

Johnny held his wrist as far away from his eyes as he could and squinted at the watch. "I don't have my glasses."

Slim looked at the watch. "I hate to leave you in a mess, but I have to be somewhere. If this pickup will start, I'm leaving."

Johnny gave his head a sad shake. "He was

always the sweetest calf."

When Slim started the pickup, we heard a high-pitched whine coming from the motor. He tried to open the crumpled hood to check it out, but the hood release was messed up.

Back inside the cab, he shook his head and growled, "That stinking buffalo mashed the fan housing and now I have to listen to that thing screech all the way home."

When we drove back to the barn, we saw Marybelle gathering up what was left of her laundry. She shot a glare at Uncle Johnny that would have skinned a hog. All at once he "thought of something he needed to do" in the corrals and vanished.

She came over and spoke to Slim. "That was a pretty fancy ride you made through my laundry."

"Sorry about that, but the power steering went out on my horse."

"Are you hurt?"

"Oh, no. It was just another day at the office."

"Well, it's a miracle. I've been telling that hard-headed old man that something like this was going to happen, and sure 'nuff, it did."

"Yes ma'am. Some men need a bigger hammer used on 'em than others. I've got a sixteen pound sledge at the ranch if you need to borrow it."

She laughed. "I may need it. Tell Loper I'll call the insurance company Monday morning and we'll make everything right. And we WILL find a new home for that buffalo!"

Slim went into the barn and led Socks outside. The horse came out looking for boogers and when he caught the scent of the buffalo, we almost had another runaway. But at last Slim got him loaded in the trailer and we began the trip back to the ranch.

For the first mile or two, he didn't say anything, but I knew it was just a matter of time. Sure enough, his eyes swung around and stabbed me. "You just had to bark, didn't you?"

Oh brother!

After a while, he grinned and chuckled under his breath. "But just between you and me, it was pretty funny, and I predict some good will come from it." He lifted a finger in the air. "I figure it'll be a long time before Loper sends me off to help Uncle Johnny with some 'little job.' Heh. Right now, old Johnny's reputation is in worse shape than mine. Or this pickup."

Okay, it was funny, just as long as he didn't try to hang all the blame on me. That happens a lot around here, you know. When anything goes wrong, blame Hank.

CHAPTER EIGHT

I Charm Some
Lady Dogs

Several miles east of Johnny's place, we reached the main highway. Slim came to a stop and we sat there for several minutes. He seemed to be lost in thought. "She sure has a pretty voice."

What? Who?

"I think I decided to marry her the first time I heard her sing 'The Water Is Wide.' Remember that?"

Oh, Viola. Of course I remembered it. She sang it at a picnic and I was sitting at her feet, staring into her eyes.

Slim smiled and sighed, then he sat up straight and glanced at the clock on the dash. "I've got an idea and I think we've got just enough time."

Instead of going east, he turned left onto the highway and picked up speed. Hmmm. This highway would take us into Twitchell, and why would we be doing that? I had been under the impression that he was in a fever to get back to the ranch so that he could make his six o'clock supper date with Viola—on time. I mean, she'd been pretty stern in telling him that if he didn't show up…she didn't say what might happen, but it seemed foolish of him to run the risk of being late.

But, of course, he didn't ask my opinion. They never do.

Fifteen minutes later, we were rolling down the main street of Twitchell, Texas. On an ordinary day, I would have been excited. If you're a ranch dog who spends most of his time out in the country, going to town is a big deal. You get to see cars and stores and people, two traffic lights, the livestock auction, the pictureshow, the saddle shop, Waterhole 83, and the Dixie Dog Drive In.

Oh, and there's always the chance that you might see some lady dogs, and that is a *very* big deal. The ladies are always impressed by a dog who cruises around town in a big three-quarter ton, four-wheel drive ranch pickup, pulling a stock trailer with a horse inside.

But as we made our way down Main Street, I noticed that people were staring at us...and laughing. And I began to understand why: *we looked ridiculous*, driving through town in that wreck of a pickup.

The hood was a rumpled mess. The door on Slim's side was smashed and we had no windshield. Lucky for us, the day had turned out fairly mild and it wasn't snowing. Even so, the wind roared through one gaping hole and back out another, causing straw and dust to swirl through the cab.

And above it all, everyone in town could hear that squeal under the hood, which sounded like a sack full of unhappy cats.

I, uh, found myself moving away from the window and shrinking down into the floorboard. I scrunched down and became an invisible dog. Slim noticed. "What's wrong with you? Are you sick?"

Yes, that was it. A touch of indigestion. Nothing major, but I felt better, uh, sitting on the floor. No kidding.

He thought about that for a moment and a grin spread across his mouth. "Are you ashamed to be seen with me?"

Well...that sounded harsh, but...yes.

He laughed. "Well, ain't you Mister High Hat! You'd better get used to this pickup, pooch, 'cause we might not get it fixed for six months. And in the meantime, don't be putting on airs." He leaned toward me. "You're just a dog."

I was aware of that.

"And you ain't Mrs. Astor's poodle."

I never pretended to be a POODLE and he didn't need to start slinging insults. Any dog with an ounce of dignity would have been embarrassed to be seen in such a junkyard pickup.

His smile faded. "Come to think of it, I've got to drive this thing down to Viola's place this evening—looking like the Grapes of Wrath. Won't her daddy be impressed?"

Exactly my point! Riding around in a junk-heap pickup was embarrassing.

In the middle of town, he pulled over to the curb and, thank goodness, shut off the noise factory. He gave me a stern glare. "Now, I've got to run into the store and get something. I won't be long, so don't wander off."

Yes sir.

He stepped out and hurried into the store. Now that the pickup motor was no longer screeching, I figured it would be safe for me to come out of hiding. I hopped up on the seat and, through the open window on the driver's side, caught sight of...my goodness, a couple of very fetching lady dogs, standing near the curb. They were talking in whispers, looking in my direction, and smiling.

Well! They'd noticed me. I moved over to the window, stuck my head outside, and gave them a chance to, you know, check out the merchandise. Heh heh. See, the ladies need time to shop, so to speak. They don't like a dog who rushes into things. You have to be patient.

I gave them several minutes to take it all in: the ears, the nose, the noble profile, the adorable eyes. Then I swung my gaze around, displayed a look of surprise, and addressed them in a sultry voice.

"Oh my. Look what I see before my very eyes, such loveliness! Have you been there long?" They giggled and nodded. "Well, do you see anything you like?"

I wiggled my left eyebrow four times. It's a little trick I learned several years ago, and it works every time. I've never figured out what's so exciting about it, but they always go for it.

Again, they giggled and whispered, then one of them said, "Would you mind if we asked you a

question?"

"Mind? Ha ha. Certainly not. In fact, I'd enjoy the challenge. What would you like to know about me? My name is Hank the Cowdog and I'm in charge of security on an enormous spread south of town, half a million acres of ranch land."

Okay, that was a slight exaggeration, but hey, I would never see these gals again, and besides, they were impressed. I mean, they gasped, so I went on.

"Ladies, I have to supervise twenty-five cowboys and ten thousand head of cattle. As you might guess, providing security for an operation of that magnetron is a daunting tisk of a task. Yes, we have savage animals on the ranch and I often find myself going into combat against them. You're probably wondering how I do it."

They giggled and whispered, then one of them said, "No, actually, we had another question."

I winked and gave them a wolfish smile. "Let me guess. You're wondering if I've ever had to go up against cattle rustlers?"

"No, we were just wondering...how many people were killed in that wreck?"

"Uh...which wreck are we talking about, my little cherry blossom?"

They looked at each other, squealed a laugh,

and said in unison, "YOUR PICKUP!"

Huh?

Never mind. You know, girl dogs who spend their entire lives in town tend to become shallow, immature, and disrespectful, and I've never cared one hoot about them. If they ever met an important dog, they'd be too dumb to know it. They're a dime a dozen and I didn't have the slightest...phooey.

I went back into hiding. My face burned, my ears burned, my reputation lay in shambles all around me. I don't know how long Slim was gone, probably not long because he hated shopping, but it seemed like hours to me.

When he climbed back into the pickup, he seemed to be in a happy mood. Good for him. I was RUINED.

He saw me huddled on the floor. "You want to see what I bought?"

No. Could we find a side street and sneak out of town?

"It ain't fancy, but it cost me a week's wages."

Great. Could we leave now?

"Don't you want to sit up in the seat and ride with the executives?"

No.

"Fine, what do I care?" He gave his head a sad

shake. "Hank, you get weirder every year."

Yes, and do you know why? *Hanging out with you!*

He turned the ignition key, unleashing the shrieks of three dozen chickens under the hood. My humiliation had surpassed the ability of language to express it. I pressed myself against the floor and tried to remember that steel endureth longer than the mud that small minds flingeth upon it.

Once we had made it out into the country, away from prying eyes and loose tongues, I sat up in the seat—confident that Slim would notice and make some smart remark. Sure enough, his eyes drifted around and landed on me.

"You know, Hank, the saddest part of this job is that we can't afford to haul you around in the kind of luxury you deserve."

I knew it. Here it came.

"I mean, a Mercedes-Benz would be about right, or maybe a Rolls Royce with bunch of chrome on the radiator. And a chauffer to open the door and feed you clams while you rode around town."

Clams. I shook my head and stared out the window. He could be so childish!

The man went on and on and wouldn't shut

up, and it got sillier by the mile. I had to listen to his mouth all the way to the ranch and I was never so glad to get out of a pickup.

Drover was sitting on the porch, in the same spot he'd been occupying when we left, and he came scampering out to meet us. I must admit that I was kind of glad to see him. He's the oddest little mutt I've ever known, but a guy can get attached to him.

While Slim unsaddled his horse and unhooked the stock trailer, Drover and I drifted toward the porch. He was hopping around like a little kangaroo, sproing, sproing, sproing. "Gosh, I'm glad you're back. Since Sally May gave me those worm pills, it gets kind of lonesome out here."

"What?"

"All my little friends are gone and I feel...I feel so all alone."

"Oh brother. Drover, please don't talk about your worms."

"We used to sing together."

I stopped and faced him. "You and your stomach worms *sang* together?"

"Oh yeah. Boy, they had the sweetest little voices! The only trouble was, they were eating me out of house and home."

"Yes, and that's why you're such a runt. They

ate you out of house and home and three years' growth."

His eyes filled with amazement. "I never thought of that. You know, I don't miss them any more. Thanks, Hank, I feel better now."

What can you say?

We continued our stroll to the porch. Since Drover had spent such a boring day, I decided to tell him about my big adventure with Uncle Johnny's buffalo.

He was amazed. "The buffalo tore down the barn, no fooling?"

"Yes sir, tore it down, laid it flat on the ground, and stomped on it. And then he ran Slim and Uncle Johnny up a tree."

Drover's eyes grew wide. "So you were all alone with the buffalo?"

"Oh yes, all alone. He turned and came at me like a train with horns."

"Oh my gosh! He honked his horns?"

"Absolutely, but it didn't do him any good. I bit him on the nose and amputated part of his ear. The big lug was so scared, he jumped up on the hood of Slim's pickup."

He twisted his head to the side. "Aw heck. I don't believe that."

"Look for yourself." I pointed to the pickup,

which was parked down by the saddle shed. Even at a distance, we could see the rumpled hood. "While he was up there, I made him do a tap dance."

Drover's eyes almost bugged out of his head. "You know, my day wasn't nearly as boring as I thought. I'm glad I stayed home."

At that moment we heard footsteps coming up behind us. It was Slim. He'd finished his chores and wore a satisfied look on his face. He stepped up on the porch and removed his chaps, then noticed Drover and me, sitting there and waiting for further orders.

"Well, dogs, I've got time to take a nice long bath. I believe this day has turned out just about perfect."

Oh yeah? Boy, was he in for a surprise!

CHAPTER NINE

Tub Time
With Slim

I wasn't sure Slim wanted us to go inside the house, but...well, every house needs a couple of dogs, right? We crept toward the door, and when he opened it, we were in position to squirt through his legs and land ourselves inside.

He growled and grumbled about "tripping over the dogs" every time he went into his house, but I knew he didn't want us wasting away on the porch.

Inside the house, he peeled off his jacket and vest and pitched them onto a chair. Then, balancing himself like a tightrope walker, he hooked the heel of his left boot into the boot jack, gave it a pull and a grunt, and slipped it off. He did the same with the other boot, stripped off his socks, and dropped them on the floor.

This was Typical Slim, dropping his socks as though they were hot coals and leaving them wherever they fell. I decided not to scold him for leaving a trail of dirty clothes all over the house. The man was old enough to know better. I mean, didn't he remember that every time a visitor came to the door, he had to run through the house, scooping up socks and underpants?

His dogs knew it, because we'd seen it happen over and over. I had a feeling that if he and Viola ever got married, she would introduce him to the dirty clothes hamper, and it wouldn't take long.

Humming a tune, he went into the bathroom and turned on the bathtub spigot. I heard his jeans hit the floor with a clunk and his shirt went flying out into the hall. A moment later, water splashed in the tub (he'd crawled into the water) and he let out a growl of satisfaction.

I turned to my assistant. "Let's move into the bathroom."

"How come?"

"Because that's where he's taking a bath."

"Yeah, but you know about me and water. I hate it."

I heaved a weary sigh. "Drover, dogs are supposed to follow their people around the house.

When they change rooms, we go with them. It's one of the things dogs have always done."

"Yeah, but what if he splashed water on us?"

"Drover, you are the most..." I rose to my feet. "Just skip it. I'm sorry I brought it up. I'll take this shift and you can stay here and...I don't know, sing to your worms."

I left the little slacker and made my way into the bathroom, where I saw Slim's face showing above the rim of the tub. His eyes were closed and he had a big smile on his face. He was submerged all the way up to his ear lobes and little plumes of steam rose out of the water. I noticed that he had left his clock sitting on the sink, where he could check the time. It said 5:03.

I stepped around his jeans (he'd dropped them right in the middle of the floor) and took up a position beside the tub. There, I sat down and gave my tail several thumps on the floor, as if to say, "Great news. I'm here!"

He heard my tail-thumps and cracked his eyes open. "Hey pooch, watch this." He made a fist with his right hand and lowered it into the water. Opening and closing his fist in the manner you would use if you were milking a cow, he caused a jet of water to go flying into the air. He looked at me and grinned. "What do think of that?"

Well, it was pretty impressive. It was something a dog could never do.

"Reckon I can hit the ceiling? I'll bet you a turkey neck I can." It took him four or five shots to do it, but by George, he actually spurted water all the way up to the ceiling, and he was proud of himself. "Heh. You owe me a turkey neck. Now, come a little closer and I'll show you another trick. You'll like this 'un."

You see what Drover was missing? He was missing out on Tub Time, one of those special events that come along without warning or planning. If you're there at the right time, you get to share precious moments with your master.

I mean, how many people or dogs in the world knew that Slim Chance could entertain himself in the bathtub by squirting water on the ceiling? Viewed from one perspective, it was kind of silly, a grown man doing such a thing, but I took a longer view, a deeper view. To me, it was one of those special Bonding Moments when I was allowed a glimpse of...

SPLAT!

...a glimpse of what a goose he could be. I couldn't believe it! You know what he did? After winning my trust and luring me closer to the tub, he turned that thing on ME and shot water in my

face!

What a cheap trick! Drover was right. Slim Chance was a joker right down to the marlowe of his bones and he just couldn't pass up an opportunity to pull childish pranks on his dogs. We give them the best years of our lives and that's what we get.

Fine. Tub Time had turned into a bitter disappointment and I dashed back into the living room. Drover was curled up in a ball and raised his head at the sound of my feet. "Oh, hi. How was it?"

"It was none of your business."

"You've got water dripping off your nose."

I held him in a steely gaze. "Drover, are you trying to make a mockery of my life?"

He grinned. "No, but I knew he'd do something. Hee hee."

"Okay, pal, you get two Chicken Marks for that. This will go into my report."

He shrugged and went back to his nap. I sat there in the middle of the room, brooding about injustice in the world and listening to the water dripping off my chin.

Ho hum. Time dragged and all at once I became aware of the ticking of the clock.

Slim needed to start getting ready. I mean, he

still had to dry off, comb his hair, jump into his clothes, and drive three miles down the creek to Viola's place. He really needed to get moving. Had he fallen asleep?

I made my way back to the bathroom. He seemed to be in a dreamy state of mind, lying there in water up to his chin. The clock said 5:20, and that made me uneasy.

Would you like to hear what he was doing? I guarantee that you won't believe this, but I was there and watched the whole thing from start to finish.

Okay, let's see if I can describe it. There he was, up to his chin in warm bathwater and humming a tune. He lifted his left foot out of the water and wiggled his toes. A grin flashed across his mouth and he moved his big toe toward the water spigot—while I watched with a rising sense of alarm.

Surely he wouldn't...this was *crazy*!

He stuck his big toe into the water spigot, into the hole where the water comes out. Five seconds later, it dawned on him that the toe was stuck and HE COULDN'T GET IT OUT!

Why would a grown man who was *supposed to be someplace in thirty minutes* stick his big toe into a water spigot?

I don't know. It defies explanation. All I can say is that if you leave Slim Chance alone in a tub, sooner or later he'll get into trouble.

What a bonehead! I could have pinched his head off.

Now what?

CHAPTER TEN

An Incredible Mess

Fellers, he'd really done it this time. The guy had survived a charging buffalo and a bronc ride through a clothesline, but this mess promised to shut him down for a long time—and probably destroy a marriage that hadn't even happened yet.

All at once, his so-called mind came roaring back to the present. He sat up in the water and moved his foot around...harder and harder...and let out a squawl of pain. "Ow!" He leaned forward and took a double hand-grip on the spigot, leaned back and...I don't know, maybe he thought he could jerk the spigot out of the wall.

Guess what, it didn't work. Duh.

Then his eyes swung around to me and (this is

a direct quote) he said, "Good honk, I can't get my toe out!"

Oh brother. You know, there are times when a dog is left speechless by the behavior of his human friends. I mean, there are people walking this earth who would say that dogs are dumb, but show me a dog who would stick his toe into a water spigot.

No dog would ever do that. No dog would even *think* about doing that.

It left me feeling so depressed, I went back into the living room. Behind me, I heard Slim yell, "Hank, don't quit me now!" I tried to push his words out of my mind, went over to the spot where Drover was napping, and woke him up.

"Drover, wake up, I have some terrible news." He sat up and I told him what had happened.

He stared at me for a long moment, then burst out laughing. "Hee hee hee. It's a joke, right?"

"I'm afraid it's not a joke, son, and we must start preparing for what comes next."

His eyes grew wide. "Gosh, what comes next?"

I swept my gaze over the ceiling. "In the Worst Case Skinnerio, Slim will sit in the bathtub for days or weeks, until someone finds him. He'll miss his date with Miss Viola and she'll figure the engagement is off. Broken-hearted, she'll move to

California, and we never see her again."

Drover almost choked on that. "Oh no! We can't let that happen!"

"Yes, well, we don't have much choice. There's nothing we can do. The man has really done it this time."

He stared at the floor and a tear rolled down his cheek. "We'll never see Viola again, ever?"

"I'm afraid that's where this is heading."

Another tear rolled down his cheek, then his eyes came up. "Wait! What if we barked?"

I studied on that. "You know, I didn't think of that. When all else fails, we should bark, right? It's worth a try. Come on, son, maybe there's still a chance!"

We dashed across the room and stood in the open door of the bathroom. Inside, we saw Slim, sitting in the tub. His face was buried in his hands and he was shaking his head and moaning, "I ain't believing this! These things just don't happen in the real world!"

I turned to Drover. "All right, soldier, begin filling your tanks." We both took deeps breath of air. "We don't have a specific bark for shattering water spigots, so punch in the All Purpose Barking Program."

"Got it. I'm ready."

"Okay, here we go. Mark and bark!"

Boy, you talk about some great barks! We leaned into the task and cut loose with round after round of deep, manly All Purpose Barks. After we had barked for about ten seconds, Slim stopped covering his face with his hands and used them to...well, to cover his ears, you might say.

And he screeched, "Dry up! I know you're trying to help, but I don't need my ears put out." The angry expression on his face melted into one of deepest despair. "What in the cat hair am I going to do!"

For a long time he sat there, groaning and shaking his head. Drover and I switched over to The Sharing of Pain. I wasn't sure it would help, but I couldn't think of a better idea.

Then Slim cut his eyes toward something on the floor. "My Leatherman's tool. It's on my belt. It's got a saw and a file." He turned his eyes on me. "Hank, you've spent most of your life being a bozo, but this time, I really need your help. Bring my pants over here!"

I turned to Drover. "What did he say?"

"Well, let me think. He's keeping a file on Bozo, but he doesn't have any pants."

"Right, that's what I heard, but it doesn't

make any sense."

Slim raised his voice. "Hank, bring my pants!"

Drover and I traded puzzled looks, and I whispered, "Something about *plants*. Maybe he wants us to water his plants."

"Yeah, but they all died 'cause nobody ever watered 'em."

"Hmm, good point."

"Maybe he said *planets*. He wants us to bark at the stars."

"Yes, but the stars won't be out for another hour."

Slim seemed to be getting more and more agitated, and he roared, "Hank, bring my pants! Bring my jeans. Blue jeans! Pants!"

Drover's eyes popped wide open. "Wait a second. His jeans are lying on the floor, right over there. Maybe he wants you to bring his pants."

"That's ridiculous. He's sitting in water and one foot's plugged into the water hydrant. There's no way he could put on his pants."

"Hank, bring my pants…now!"

My mind was racing. "Wait, hold everything. He wants me to *bring his pants*."

"I'll be derned."

"And I think I can do it. Stand by." I marched over to the jeans sprawled in the middle of the floor and gave them a sniffing. Hmm, horse sweat.

"Hank, hurry up! It's almost six o'clock!"

For a man who was in a helpless situation, he sure didn't waste much time on manners. I mean, you'd think he could have spoken in a civil tone and maybe even said "please."

Oh well. I fitted my jaws around the jeans and dragged them over to the tub. Slim raised himself off the bottom of the tub and leaned out as far as he could, until he managed to snatch one of the pant legs. And he started pulling.

I had my jaws clamped down on the belt-region. Slim pulled and I pulled, and all at once I understood. *He wanted to play Tug!*

Well, that was okay with me. I mean, it seemed a strange thing to be doing, but we dogs are often called upon to do things that don't...

Good grief, he snatched the jeans right out of my mouth, and almost took my teeth along for the ride! Hey, take it easy with the teeth, pal, or you'll end up playing Tug by yourself!

He wasn't paying any attention to me. His trembling hands went to the leather case on his belt and he came up holding something made of shiny metal. Okay, it was his Leatherman's tool and maybe that's what he'd been wanting all along. But why hadn't he just said so? I mean, how's a dog supposed to know?

He fumbled around with the device and brought out a little saw, about three inches long. He leaned forward and started sawing on...was he going to cut off his toe? I looked closer. No, he was sawing the spigot, about an inch above the end of his toe.

Well, good. A guy should never cut off his toe until he's tried everything else.

He sawed and he sawed, and finally gave up. "It won't cut metal." He fumbled around with the tool again and brought out another attachment, a little file. Again, he went to work.

I don't know how long he scraped with the file, but it seemed hours. At last, he leaned back in the tub and stared straight ahead with a look of total defeat in his eyes.

"It would take me a month to file that thing off. It can't be done. I'm whipped. I've lost Viola and I guess I'll die in my own bathtub. Two months from now, they'll find my bones."

Well, you can imagine what an effect those words had on little Mister Squeakbox. His eyes almost bugged out of his head. "Oh my gosh, I'm scared of skeletons!"

He started running in circles, dashed out into

the hall, made a right turn, and headed for the bedroom as fast as his legs would carry him. I didn't actually see him crawl under Slim's bed, but I knew that's where he went.

He always crawls under the bed when Life veers out of control.

Well, Life had certainly veered out of control, and I must admit that I was having my own struggle with panic. Think about it. I was twenty-five miles from town, locked in a house where people seldom came to visit, and *the only human on the place had his big toe stuck in a bathtub spigot.*

Should I follow Drover's example and hide under the bed? It was tempting, I won't deny it, but sometimes a dog has to choose between what is comfortable and what is RIGHT.

No sir, I wouldn't leave my cowboy. When darkness came and the fire went out in the stove, we would shiver together in a cold house and listen to our stomachs growling. We would grow old together and turn into skeletons together, and when they found our bones, they would know that Hank the Cowdog had remained faithful to the bitter...

Huh?

Did you hear that? Maybe not, because you

weren't there, but I sure heard it. Would you like to guess what it might have been? Here are some possibilities:

The house was on fire.

A water pipe had burst under the kitchen sink.

We were having an earthquake.

Wolf Creek was flooding and water was pouring into the living room

Termites were eating the house and the roof was about to collapse.

A rabid skunk had entered the room.

It sounds pretty grim, doesn't it? But you should always remember the wise old saying: "It's always darkest before it gets any darker."

Hang on.

CHAPTER ELEVEN

The Second Ring

Okay, maybe I cheated a little bit. See, I listed some awful things that *could* have happened, but not the one that *did* happen. Here's what actually happened.

Somebody was knocking on the door!

My eyes and Slim's eyes met. "Hank, don't let 'em leave! Bark, let 'em know we're in here!"

Aye aye, sir! I flew out of the...BONK...ran into the door frame, I mean, my back legs were moving so fast on the limoleun floor, I lost control there for a second, but I'm no quitter. I got things straightened out and headed for the front door. There, I fired off several blasts of barking that said, "Hey, we're trapped in here and have a man down, repeat, MAN DOWN!"

The knocking stopped. I cocked my ear and listened. The doorknob squeaked and began to turn, and you know, up until that very moment, I hadn't considered the possibility that whoever was out there might be...well, a burglar or even a Charlie Monster. Don't forget, those guys are clever beyond our wildest dreams and they use all kinds of disguises to...

The hinges gave an eerie squeak and the crack in the door widened, and all at once, there stood A MAN. Evening shadows concealed his face...or maybe he didn't have a face. You know, vampires can erase their faces and...huge fangs, dripping with fresh blood?

Fellers, my hair bristled up and I began...

"Where's Slim? Slim? Hey, what happened to the hood of my pickup?"

Holy smokes, it was Loper! Oh happy day! You thought he was a vampire, right? Ha ha. Even I was fooled there for a second. Boy, those shadows and a squeaky hinge will play tricks on your mind.

Slim's voice boomed from the back of the house. "I'm in here!"

Loper brushed past me and headed for the bathroom. In the doorway, he stopped and stared at the scene inside. "What in the world..."

"Loper, I'm in a mess and I'll tell you all about it later, but right now, go down to the shed. There's a hacksaw hanging on the wall. Bring it and that package of fresh blades too. You'll need a bunch of sharp blades."

A smirkle ripped across Lippers lopes... Loper's liver...Liver's lips...phooey. A smirk rippled across Loper's lips, and he said, "Your toe's stuck in the spigot?"

"What do you think? Yes! *Get the saw and hurry!*

Loper studied the situation for a moment, rubbing his chin and narrowing his eyes. Then he left the room. He came back with a squeeze bottle of liquid soap. "Before I tear up the plumbing and cut off your toe, let me try something else."

"It won't work. Hurry up! I'm supposed to be somewhere and I'm an hour late."

Loper removed his hat and brought a finger to his lips. "Shhh. We have a great mind at work in this house. Try to keep your big mouth shut and let me concentrate." He leaned over the edge of the tub and squeezed soap up into the faucet. "Try it now."

Slim tugged with his foot and shook his head. "It's swole up. Get the saw."

Loper set the bottle on the floor and placed both

hands on Slim's ankle. "Close your eyes and think about the first time you ate chocolate ice cream."

"Uh uh! Loper, don't..." In a flash, Loper shoved down on the foot, hard and fast. There was a crunching sound and a big splash Slim squawled in pain. "OW! You tore it plumb off!"

He raised his foot out of the water, and by George, the toe was still attached, and it had a real pretty red ring around it.

Loper straightened up and shook his head. "You are such a baby. Now tell me how it happened."

"I ain't talking. You'd just say it was stupid."

"Oh, I will not. Scout's Honor."

"Promise you won't tell anyone?"

"Slim, what goes on in your bathroom *stays* in your bathroom."

"Well..." He blinked his eyes. "I just wondered if I could stick my toe in there."

"That's it?" Loper cackled. "That's the stupidest thing I ever heard. I can't wait to tell Sally May. Ha ha ha!"

"Loper, you're a rat, but I don't have time to talk about it."

Slim leaped out of the tub, wrapped himself in a towel, and dripped and hobbled into the bedroom, where he started jumping into his clothes.

Loper followed. "Where are you going in such

a rush? It must be pretty important. I've never seen you move so fast."

"I've got a date."

"With a human being?"

"With Viola, if she's still there."

Slim limped past Loper, gave him a glare, and went into the bathroom. Standing in front of the mirror, he raked his hair with a brush and started building a knot in his necktie.

Loper watched. "How's the toe?"

"It hurts, what do you think? You pret' near jerked it out by the roots."

"What if you can't get your boot on?"

Slim hadn't thought of that. He stared at himself in the mirror. "I'll wear a house shoe."

Loper shook his head and chuckled. "Are you going to tell her what happened?"

"Loper, just hush. I don't know what I'll tell her. I take life one wreck at a time."

"Speaking of wrecks, what did you do to my pickup?"

Slim talked while he tossed his tie into a knot. "That 'calf' Uncle Johnny told you about? It was a fifteen hundred pound buffalo bull, and he spent some time walking around on the hood of your pickup. Laugh about *that*."

Loper's smile dropped like a dead bird.

Slim hobbled back into the bedroom and rummaged through the closet until he found his dress boots, a nice pair of black bull-hides that he wore to church and funerals. He pulled on the right one without much effort, but the left one didn't fit his swollen toe. He slipped his bad foot into a sheepskin slipper, pulled on his suit jacket, and showed himself to Loper.

"What do you think?"

Loper looked him over. "Ugly suit, crooked tie, old house shoe. Nice. Viola's a lucky woman." He gave Slim a pat on the shoulder and left. As he went out the door, he yelled, "I'll send you a bill for the toe."

Slim put me and Drover outside, grabbed his banjo case, closed up the house, and hurried to his pickup, limping on his bad foot.

We dogs sat on the porch and watched. Drover gave his head a shake. "What if Viola got mad and left?"

I had been worrying about that too. "Then Slim will lose the best thing that ever walked into his life."

"I kind of wish we could go with him."

"I agree. If there was ever a time when he needed the support of his dogs, this is it."

Slim started the pickup and we heard the

squeal come from under the hood. "Gosh, I think he just ran over a cat."

"No, it's some problem with the motor and... why are you staring at me?"

"I just thought of something. If Slim needs our help, why don't we go with him?"

"Because..." I rose to my feet. "Good point. We'll have to jump into the back while the pickup's moving. Can you do it?"

Drover leaped to his feet and his eyes glowed with determination. "Oh yeah, I can do this!"

"Well, let's go!"

We dived off the porch and raced after the pickup. It was moving but hadn't gained much speed, and I noticed that Slim wasn't looking into his side mirror. Do you know why? Because Winkie Buffalo had removed it.

I went flying into the back as gracefully as a deer, then looked back to check on Drover. He was falling behind. He slowed, stopped, waved goodbye, and went back to the porch.

Oh well, at least one of us from the Security Division would be there to help Slim through his time of greatest need.

But it was too soon to celebrate. Don't forget: We still didn't know if Viola would be there.

CHAPTER TWELVE

The Third Ring

I wasted no time moving myself to the front of the pickup bed, where I crouched down behind the cab. I didn't think there was much chance that Slim would check to see if he was hauling dogs, but a guy never knows. Just when you think he doesn't notice anything, he notices something.

It was a short three-mile drive down the Wolf Creek road to the old two-story house where Miss Viola stayed with her aging parents. When we pulled up in front of the house, the pickup was making even more noise than before, which is really saying something.

Here's how noisy it was. When we arrived at the house, Viola's two dogs, Black and Jack, came rushing out, barking their heads off and talking all kinds of trash, but when they heard the squeals and shrieks coming from the motor, they did a one-eighty and vanished into the chinaberry grove behind the house.

They didn't know what we had under the hood, and they wanted no part of it.

Or...wait, I just thought of this. Maybe they caught sight of ME in the back of the pickup and, you know, decided that they wanted no part of what I usually dish out to mouthy ranch mutts. That makes sense, doesn't it? You bet.

So, yes, they took one look at me and ran for their lives. I was tempted to chase them down and give them the thrashing they so richly deserved, but, well, Slim and I had important business and I decided to let it slide.

You might say that the squeal of the pickup motor announced our presence. By the time Slim had gotten out and limped his way to the house, the porch light snapped on, the door opened, and out stepped an elderly, stern-faced man with white hair and suspenders on his pants.

Woodrow, Viola's daddy.

He shaded his eyes with a hand and studied Slim with a suspicious look. "What's all the noise?"

"Evening, Woodrow, it's me."

"Who's me? I can't see a thing." He snapped on a flashlight and turned it on Slim's face. "Oh. How come you're dressed up? You going to a funeral?"

"I hope not. I came to see Viola."

"Well, you're too late. She's gone."

"Gone!"

"Yes sir, we'd just sat down for supper. She jumped out of her chair and left the house, crying. I don't know what got into her head."

"Any idea where she might have gone?"

Woodrow gave his head a shake. "She took her mandolin. Maybe she ran off and joined the circus. What's wrong with your foot?"

"Horse stepped on it."

"Well, if she ever comes back, I'll tell her you were here." He went back into the house and closed the door.

Slim's shoulders sagged and he stood there for a long time, staring at the ground. Then I heard him say in a croaking voice, "I guess it wasn't meant to be."

He started back to the pickup, walking like a crippled old man, but then he stopped and listened. He'd heard something. I'd heard it too. Music, some kind of instrument. It seemed to be coming from the barn.

Somebody was inside the barn, playing a mandolin! Could it be...

Slim's face lit up. He reached into the pickup and brought out his banjo case, then headed for the barn, walking as fast as he could on his bad foot.

I slithered myself off the back of the pickup and followed along behind.

He peeked through the window, gave his head a nod, and went inside. When he'd gone, I took his place and looked through the window. There, I saw Miss Viola, sitting by herself on a bale of wheat straw, surrounded by an old John Deere tractor, an army surplus Jeep, and her daddy's Massy-Harris hay baler.

She was playing Slim's favorite song on the mandolin, "The Water Is Wide." Oh, and I noticed that her eyes were red-rimmed, a sure sign that she'd been crying. I wanted to rush to her side and give her comfort, but didn't dare.

She was so absorbed in her playing, she didn't notice Slim. He opened up his banjo case, pulled out the instrument, sat down on a bale of straw, and began playing along with her. They did the whole song and it sure was nice. Viola had the sweetest soprano voice I'd ever heard.

When it was over, she lifted her gaze and stared at him. "I thought you weren't coming."

"Viola, I had some trouble and got here as quick as I could. Honest."

"But why didn't you call? Slim Chance, I've just spent the most miserable one hour of my entire life! And the whole time, I was thinking...I won't even tell you what I was thinking."

"I know. I'm sorry."

She stared at the floor. "Mom and Daddy went ahead and ate. The supper's cold...everything's turned into a mess!"

"Well, not everything. I'm here and you're here, and I'm fixing to sing you a song."

She looked at him for a long moment. "You're going to sing me a song?"

He wasn't kidding. Remember that pretty song he'd done for us dogs earlier in the day? Well, he sang it for her, right there in the barn. "Viola's Song." Should we listen to it? Let's do.

Viola's Song

I'm sitting here drinking my coffee.
It rained in the night and more's on the way.
The fog hugs the tops of the caprock.
This valley is looking like heaven today.

The horse pasture's covered with winecups.
They're purple and perfect and covered with dew.
What I see with my eyes are the flowers,
But Viola, I'm thinking of you.

That flat by the creek is a-blazing
With colors of orange and yellow and red.
It's the flower we call Indian Paintbrush.
There's a bunch of 'em down by the saddle shed.

The air's filled with fragrance of grapevines,
Fresh grass and sagebrush and things that are new.
I'm amazed by the work of the Maker.
And Viola, I'm thinking of you.

God gave us this morning in Texas,
My spirit is nourished and blessed by the view.
There's only one thing I could ask for:
Viola, to share it with you.

What did I tell you? Not bad, huh? Who
would have thought that a goof-off like Slim
Chance could come up with a tender love song—
and perform it in a barn! I mean, I'd heard plenty
of his songs and they were about what you'd
expect from a guy who drives around in a pickup

and sings to his dogs. Not so great. Corny.

But this one revealed a side of him I hadn't seen before, and neither had Viola. She listened to every word, and even played along with him. By the end of the song, tears were sliding down her cheeks.

Silence filled the barn. As if on cue, they both put their instruments in their cases, met in the middle, wrapped their arms around each other, and swayed back and forth for a long time.

At last Viola said, "It's a beautiful song and it says so much about the good heart of the man who wrote it."

Slim swallowed a lump in his throat. "Reckon you could marry him?"

She looked into his eyes. "Of course I will, you big lug! You're all I've ever wanted, but I thought you'd changed your mind." She buried her face in his chest. "I'm so glad you didn't!"

"Me too, and I'm glad you didn't run off and join the circus."

She wiped her eyes and looked at the slipper on his foot. "What happened to your foot?"

He heaved a sigh. He knew this was going to be a long story, so he told her to sit down. He joined her on a bale of straw and told her all about his day: Uncle Johnny, Winkie, the famous bronc ride through Aunt Marybelle's clothesline, and Winkie trampling the hood of the pickup.

She was astounded, laughing one minute and gasping the next. Then he got to the part about sticking his toe into the bathtub spigot. She listened in stunned silence, shaking her head. "There are things about cowboys that I might never understand."

He rose from the bale of hay and held himself erect. "Me too. Well, let's go break the bad news to your folks."

He offered his hand and helped her up. "Did you remember to bring the...well, the lock washer?"

Slim snapped his fingers and scowled. "Darn. I forgot it."

"Slim! How could you forget the ring?"

He gave her a wink and a grin, and pulled a little box out of his pocket. He flipped it open and showed her a real, genuine engagement ring. So that's why he'd made the trip into town! The tiny diamond didn't have much sparkle, but her eyes made up for it. They lit up like the biggest, prettiest diamonds in the world.

Arm in arm, they left the barn and guess who was waiting outside. Me. I was prouder of Slim than I'd ever been in my whole life, and more in

love with Viola than ever before, but I didn't throw myself into her arms or jump up on Slim's clean suit.

They were surprised to see me, and Slim couldn't resist grumbling about "disobedient dogs." At the yard gate, he stopped. "This is as far as you go, pooch. Get in the pickup. If Woodrow goes for his gun, I'll be right out."

Viola laughed and pulled Slim toward the house. "Come on, cowboy, this won't be as bad as you think."

They went inside and left me alone. I jumped the fence, sprinted across the yard, and took up a position at one of the living room windows. I mean, how many times does a dog get to see something like this? Hey, I had the rest of my life to sit in the pickup and be a good dog.

Viola's parents sat on a big sofa, and Viola and Slim stood in front of them, holding hands. Through the window glass, I heard Slim's voice— his trembling voice. "Woodrow, I'm here to ask permission to marry your daughter."

Viola's mother let out a gasp and covered her mouth with her hand. Woodrow looked as though he'd swallowed a pickle. Then he roared, "That is the dumbest thing I ever heard! How can you support a wife on cowboy wages?"

Slim straightened his back and raised his voice. "By grabs, I'll do it the same way you done it. I'll work hard and do whatever it takes, and I guarantee that she'll be cared for."

The old man's eyes flicked back and forth from one to the other. "Viola, daughter, is this what you want, or did he fast-talk you into it?"

Her eyes sparkled. "Daddy, this is what I've wanted since the first day I met him, and I thought he'd never ask. Everything's going to be all right."

Woodrow shook his head and muttered under his breath. Viola's mother started crying. Wow, things didn't look so great, but then Woodrow pushed himself up from the sofa, hugged his daughter, and offered Slim his hand. "Well, God looks after fools, and He'll sure stay busy looking after y'all two."

Slim pulled out the engagement ring. "Viola, will you marry me?"

A sly twinkle came into her eyes. "Can I have a few months to think about it?"

"No ma'am, you sure can't."

"In that case...YES, I WILL MARRY YOU, SLIM CHANCE!"

He slipped the ring on her finger and they flew into each other's arms. Old Woodrow was still shaking his head and Viola's mom was still crying, but maybe they were happy tears.

Holy smokes, what a finish! And now you understand the mystery of the Three Rings. The first was a lock washer, the second the red ring around Slim's big toe, and the third a genuine engagement ring that he finally managed to get on Viola's finger.

Whew! What an ordeal! Broncs, buffaloes, and bathtubs. I thought I'd never get things straightened out.

But wait. Did they ever get married? Heh. That's another story.

This case is closed.

Have you read all
of Hank's adventures?

Join Hank the Cowdog's Security Force

Are you a big Hank the Cowdog fan? Then you'll want to join Hank's Security Force! Here is some of the neat stuff you will receive:

Welcome Package
- A Hank paperback
- An Original (19"x25") Hank Poster
- A Hank bookmark

Eight digital issues of
The Hank Times **with**
- Lots of great games and puzzles
- Stories about Hank and his friends
- Special previews of future books
- Fun contests

More Security Force Benefits
- Special discounts on Hank books, audios, and more
- Special Members-Only section on website

Total value of the Welcome Package and *The Hank Times* is $23.99. However, your two-year membership is **only $7.99** plus $5.00 for shipping and handling.

☐ Yes I want to join Hank's Security Force. Enclosed is $12.99 ($7.99 + $5.00 for shipping and handling) for my **two-year membership**. [Make check payable to Maverick Books.]

Which book would you like to receive in your Welcome Package? (#_____) any book except #50

                                                BOY or GIRL

YOUR NAME   (CIRCLE ONE)

MAILING ADDRESS

CITY   STATE   ZIP

TELEPHONE   BIRTH DATE

E-MAIL   (required for digital Hank Times)

Send check or money order for $12.99 to:

Hank's Security Force
Maverick Books
PO Box 549
Perryton, Texas 79070

DO NOT SEND CASH. NO CREDIT CARDS ACCEPTED.
Allow 2–3 weeks for delivery.
Offer is subject to change.

The following activity is a sample from *The Hank Times*, the official newspaper of Hank's Security Force. Please do not write on this page unless this is your book. Even then, why not just find a scrap of paper?

For more games and activities like this one, as well as up-to-date news about upcoming Hank books, be sure to check out Hank's official website at **www.hankthecowdog.com**!

"Photogenic" Memory Quiz

We all know that Hank has a "photogenic" memory—being aware of your surroundings is an important quality for a Head of Ranch Security. Now you can test your powers of observation.

How good is your memory? Look at the illustration on page 13 and try to remember as many things about it as possible. Then turn back to this page and see how many questions you can answer.

1. Was the picture shape a *Square, Rectangle, or Oval*?

2. Which of Slim's feet could you see? HIS *Left or Right*?

3. Was Drover looking *Up, Down, or Straight Ahead*?

4. Which of Hank's ears could you see? *HIS Left or Right*?

5. What appliance was in the back room? *Furnace, Oven, or Microwave?*

6. How many of Slim's hands could you see? *0, 1, 2, or all 3*?

"Word Maker"

Try making words from the names below. Make up to twenty words with as many letters as possible.

Then, count the total number of letters used in all of the words you made. See how well you did using the security rankings below.

UNCLE   JOHNNY

59-61 You spend too much time with J.T. Cluck and the chickens.

62-64 You are showing some real Security Force potential.

65-68 You have earned a spot on our ranch security team.

69+ Wow! You rank up there as a top-of-the-line cowdog.

Photo Courtesy of Western Horseman Magazine

John R. Erickson, a former cowboy, has written numerous books for both children and adults and is best known for his acclaimed *Hank the Cowdog* series. He lives and works on his ranch in Perryton, Texas, with his family.

Gerald L. Holmes has illustrated numerous cartoons and textbooks in addition to the *Hank the Cowdog* series. He lives in Perryton, Texas.

Shawn Tevis Photography

31901055694642